FOOL ME THRICE

Money Changes Everything

∾

BY : DEAN CONAN

CONTENTS

ACKNOWLEDGMENTS 1

INTRODUCTION 3

CHAPTER ONE 7

CHAPTER TWO 11

CHAPTER THREE 19

CHAPTER FOUR 33

CHAPTER FIVE 37

CHAPTER SIX 49

CHAPTER SEVEN 61

CHAPTER EIGHT 69

CHAPTER NINE 79

CHAPTER TEN 93

CHAPTER ELEVEN 103

CHAPTER TWELVE 117

CHAPTER THIRTEEN 131

CHAPTER FOURTEEN 139

CHAPTER FIFTEEN 149

CHAPTER SIXTEEN 159

CHAPTER SEVENTEEN 169

CHAPTER EIGHTEEN 175

CHAPTER NINETEEN 189

CHAPTER TWENTY 199

CHAPTER TWENTY-ONE 213

CHAPTER TWENTY-TWO 223

CHAPTER TWENTY-THREE 231

CHAPTER TWENTY-FOUR 241

CHAPTER TWENTY-FIVE 255

ABOUT THE AUTHOR 263

ACKNOWLEDGMENTS

I want to thank my mother for being the inspiration for everything I wanted to be.

I want to thank Lamont Ingram for his wit, wisdom, and professionalism that kept me going.

Finally, I want to thank God for giving me the creativity to bring my visions, humor, and fantasies to books.

INTRODUCTION

No doubt, I was born a sucker—a sucker for a big booty and a smile that is. I have to admit I was abused by each and every gold-digger I came across.

For as long as I can remember, I've chased after the kitty, and it took me losing all my belongings to realize I had a problem.

I've never really been in love, at least, I don't think I have. The only woman I can for sure say ever loved me is my mom. Yes, I've had some childhood friends where the bonds ran deep, but that was it.

Growing up, Mom and Dad owned The Fuller Funeral Parlor. It was the most successful Mortuary in Houston, Texas. That meant a whole lot of business. It was damn good for us but not so good for the families of the dead.

We were wealthy. Some would even say rich. Yet, everybody around town knew it too. My folks built this enormous house for just the three of us right across from the family's parlor.

My dad, Charles Fuller, had been one smooth mortician. He was the best in the business and damn good at his job. But his role as a husband and father was of lesser importance. He loved us. We knew that. But he loved the dead and his money even more. Moments with him were rare and precious memories are few.

Dean Conan

Luckily, my mom made sure she gave me enough love for the both of them. She reminded me to stay human while dad's primary focus was preparing the dead and grooming me for the day that I would take over. Still, I wasn't even close to being ready as the heir to the Fuller's empire. Such is life for a brat like me.

On the night of my high school graduation, my mom and dad were killed in a car accident. To add to my trauma, the drunk driver just happened to be my high school nemesis, Dickie Beale. Dickie was always a hater because all the girls chased after me instead of him.

Dickie's family had a little bit more money than we had at the time. Throw in a shit load of connection and political favors, and Dickie Beale got off with only losing his license with some minor probations. *Son of a bitch.*

That was it. My folks were gone, and for the first time, I was all alone. Well, that's if you didn't count the millions, the house, the wagons, and the dead bodies that were left for me.

Preparing my parents for burial was the first time I truly appreciated my dad's profession. It allowed me to experience why my father loved it so much. Even though I was screwed up emotionally, dressing my folks for their final rest was one of my greatest accomplishments. I remember putting a smile on my father's face. Literally. It was the first time he wore a smile outside of work.

My mother looked at peace. No longer did she have to worry about my dad or me. No longer did she have to worry about the girls chasing behind me. Mom had definitely made her mark. Yet, I didn't realize how important she was to my everyday life until she was no longer there.

Fool Me Thrice

I had more money than I knew what to do with. I had no one around to remind me that the love of money was nowhere near as important as true love itself. Needless to say, it didn't take long for my life to spiral out of control.

Chapter ONE

Dean Conan

I was known as Charlie Mo for "Charles The Mortician." Since I'm known as a Bona Fide Asshole, I'm sure many use my name "Charlie Mo" as a way to call me "Charles The Moron," but that doesn't bother me. Only haters use insults to hide their envy anyway. Mom actually named me Prince Charles Fuller. She had this thing for the Royal family of England. There is no other like me, so I love being called Charlie Mo. It is an honor to my mom and dad.

As long as I can remember, only the needy came around. If they didn't have two open hands, then they had even bigger sad ass stories. Gold-diggers flocked around me like a moth to a flame and bees to a sweet honeycomb. I was their honey with a bank account full of money. I was their dream come true. Or, more like their payday to the rescue.

At first, I didn't care. I saw it as a small price for what I wanted. Many would often say they loved me, but I knew they really didn't. I didn't care, though. I genuinely felt like I had the juice. I felt like I was on top of the world. I was living life like a king. But even kings have responsibilities.

Most days, work was the last thing on my mind. It would not have taken a genius to predict my destruction. With all my focus being on cars, money, and wild ass women, the parlor business began to fail.

With me in charge, the Fuller Funeral Home stayed on life support. I was too distracted for business and too determined to be with the next girl. No doubt, I wasn't nearly as good with the parlor as my pops had been. My incompetence buried the family good image almost overnight.

Many so-called friends, relatives, and professionals did try to help. They tried to guide me, but I trusted no one. In my mind, they all wanted something because they always have. That's exactly what mom taught me.

Fool Me Thrice

She told me about the relatives and friends she lost because she wouldn't be their piggy bank. She barely spoke to many in her family because they always acted as if she owed them something. They felt she had it to give, and they expected her to give it. She told me freeloaders would always expect the same from me. She said, "You need to drop any and all associations with people like that. I didn't need anyone like that in my life, no matter who they were."

Boy, was mama right. Amazing how those users would try to guilt me with religion or some type of morals if I didn't grant them money. They would pick verses out of the Bible as a way to separate me from my inheritance. It would be, "The Lord said, give and it will be given to you." If I did loan out anything, then I was supposed to wait for God to pay me back. Wow! Or, if I said, "no" to their requests, then it would be, "Charlie Mo, you gonna miss your blessing."

Truthfully, I was already blessed. My mom and dad had already favored me with a hell of a lot. But I did need someone. I needed help. I just didn't realize it until it was far too late.

Dean Conan

Chapter TWO

Dean Conan

Being that my money was funny, I had to find a job and work like all the other living stiffs. With no experience, it took a while but fortunately, The Houston City Sanitation Department took a chance on me.

Most of the time, I kept to myself, yet many of the workers knew my family or had seen me at the parlor. I could tell none of them really knew what to make of Charlie Mo. They had all heard the rumors of my demise, but none of them cared to believe I was really out of money. All the fellas still asked me for loans and cash advances. But whenever I said "no" or "I'm broke," they just assumed I was putting them off.

Those idiots always ridiculed me. They made snide remarks like, "Charlie Mo has No Dead Benjamins" or "No Cold Cash on Charlie Mo," or "Charlie Mo The Undertaker has no Green Paper."

My days were long and alone. The pay was little, but I kept on pushing. Because I needed a little extra money, I auctioned off things I had of value until I barely had anything left.

My mom and dad would be so ashamed of me for losing everything they'd worked so hard to build and maintain. I never learned anything about making sacrifices. My folks sheltered me and didn't prepare me for the real world.

I was never the labor type but working at Houston City Sanitation gave me an appreciation of having a good honest job. That was a really good thing for me. It left me very little time to think and feel sorry for myself because pity doesn't pay the bills. On a good note, Dad did manage to teach me not to be afraid to stand out. So, I worked hard and was determined to be the best.

Fool Me Thrice

My manager, Tin-Can Stan, had taken notice. He even told me I might become the head foreman in record time provided I kept up the pace and continued to be work reliable. I knew for sure the rest of the fellas would have a lot to say about that. Being promoted would kill the hopes of a lot of my lazy peers.

Tin-Can Stan had been with Houston City Sanitation for about fifteen years. He began as a journeyman, my current position. When he started, most of the clients still had metal trash cans. Stan was notorious for being the noisiest worker. His singing and clanging of the cans earned him the name Tin-Can Stan.

At that time, he was a manager and the coordinator of our crew. He never left the truck to made collections, but he still sang and annoyed the workers on ride-a-longs. Tin-Can was also a no-bullshit type of boss. He pushed us to perform, rarely allowed breaks, and watched our every move. He wasn't very well-liked by most of the workers, but he didn't bother me.

My parents weren't the social type, but something told me Tin-Can knew my folks even though they may not have known him. The day I came to apply for the job, Tin-Can was there and appeared to be really good with the people in Human Resources. I wouldn't be surprised if Tin-Can had a say with HCS's decision to hire me.

"How you doin' today, son?"

For some reason, I thought it would bother me for Tin-Can to call me "son," but it didn't.

"I'm making it, sir."

"I picked these up last night. You goin' through those cheap work gloves every week. These should last you a while," Tin-Can said while handing me a different brand of mittens.

Tin-Can was a big, tall man, weighing around two hundred pounds. He was light-skinned and always kept a bald head, a big beard, and a pair of glasses on his face or in his pocket. He had to be about the same age as my dad would have been, somewhere in his late forties.

"Aw man, you didn't have to do that. How much do I owe you?"

Tin-Can placed his hand on my shoulder. "Funny," he said while walking away.

They were some damn good ones. I made a mental note to bring Tin-Can a bottle of my dad's exotic whiskeys that were left behind to show my appreciation. I hadn't been much of a drinker since my parents' death, but I had a whole closet full of spirits.

After a long day of work, I always tried to wind down and plan a way forward. My apartment was small, but it was all I needed. The rooms were jammed with a lot of family belongings. I was never the packrat, but I couldn't let go of my parents' souvenirs.

I walked into the spare bedroom to retrieve a bottle of liquor for Tin-Can out of the closet and stopped to look around at some of my folks' treasured collections. Most of the items in that room had sentimental value. I would never even think about trying to sell most of those things, no matter how broke I was.

I noticed a box of cigars that belonged to my dad on the top shelf. Even though I could have probably gotten a pretty penny for those smokes, I refused to let his stogies go.

Pops used to smoke half a cigar every time he finished preparing a body for burial. It was his "good job" reward to himself. If the accident hadn't gotten him, I'm positive lung cancer would've found him soon.

Fool Me Thrice

As soon as I sniffed the box, I could see him just rocking back and forth in his favorite car with his eyes closed. He wasn't around much, but I still miss him. I miss the look on mama's face when he finally decided to walk across the street and come home. I miss how he would call my name and the stories he would tell about the dead people he worked on.

Daddy didn't know most of the corpses he dressed for burial, but he would still make up tales about how they died. To the younger me, I always thought his stories were real. Once I got older, I realized it was just a part of his vision. It helped him decide what they would look like when they were presented to their families.

"Damn!"

The box dropped from my hands as I tried to put them back in place on the shelf. The cigars rolled around on the floor as two unopened envelopes lay still right by my feet.

"What the hell is this?"

One envelope had my name on the front and the other... *Boy! How the hell did I forget about this?* While ignoring the letter addressed to me, I opened the most important envelope -- the one about *my* trust fund.

✦✦✦

Feeling good about my countdown to millionaire status, I decided to get up and get dressed to go to the gym. I threw on my black Nike outfit and matching shoes. The weather was nice, so I opted to jog instead of drive. I hadn't been working out as I should, so I was long overdue for an outdoor run.

Dean Conan

As I jogged to the gym, I thought about how much my life would change on my birthday. I was going to be a millionaire…again. I had screwed up everything before and didn't want to do that again. Tin-Can was cool, but I didn't want to work at HCS if I didn't have to.

I rounded the corner and saw that the parking lot in front of the gym was packed. It was the typical after-work rush, so I had to make sure that I hopped on the first open bench I could find. No sooner than I grabbed my dumbbells and sat down, I heard this sultry voice in my ear.

"Well, hello, stranger."

I could pinpoint that voice anywhere. It could be no other woman than Chardonnay. Chardonnay was a woman I came across over three years ago when I was on a Californian wine tour.

She started out so sweet and delicate. She was as tempting as seasonal fruit. At first, she joked about how young I was when I came on to her. But once she saw my car, she started singing a different tune.

She appeared to be so genuine and a romantic dream. Chardonnay had a son and a daughter from a previous relationship. Fooling around with her became a balancing act of dating and being a nanny. All of our outings had to include Chardonnay's two kids, according to her.

Well, I was going to follow that body regardless of what it took. But for a minute, the little ones did make me feel kinda…*normal*. Yeah, that's the word. It felt like my own little family, even though Chardonnay was just another one of my *bones*.

Everything unraveled when I got wind that Chardonnay's prison stopovers to see her father were actually conjugal visits to her babies' daddy. She was using my money to put on his books. So, I was taking care of her, her kids, and some dude with ten years left in prison.

She didn't expect me to find out. But once I did, Chardonnay tried to sell me the notion of being all he had. How in the hell was that my problem? So, just like that, Chardonnay was cut off from the Charlie Mo Gravy Train.

All I had left to offer her was half of a smile. I picked up my weights and started my first set of bicep curls. Looking in the mirror in front of me, I couldn't help but watch her walk away. She looked amazing, but I wasn't going down that road again with Chardonnay. She was bad news with criminal baggage.

Dean Conan

Chapter THREE

The next day, I arrived to work a few minutes early with plans of putting the bottle of whiskey in Tin-Can's locker. However, he was already at the table drinking his morning brew.

Tin-Can smiled at me. "Good morning, son. What do you have there?"

"A little something from my dad's stash. Thank you for the gloves."

I thought he was going to shake my hand, but instead, he stood up and pulled me in for an embrace. It had been quite a while since I'd gotten a genuine hug from anyone, especially from a father-like figure. Pops would give me high-fives all the time. The last time he actually embraced me was the day he died – my graduation day. With a hug, dad told me he loved me and was proud of me.

"It's no problem," I said as I pulled away from Tin-Can.

He was so overjoyed that he asked me to break the seal with him after work. I told him I had plans, but he went even further and invited me over for dinner. I didn't want to go, but I didn't want to insult him either. I was used to my own solitude, plus getting closer to Tin-Can would drive a bigger wedge between my co-workers and me. I was sure of it. But what the hell. Those guys weren't going to accept me anyway unless I was giving them money. So, I accepted Tin-Can's offer.

After work, I rushed home and showered so that I could stop by the store to pick up some of those homemade baked cookies I was sure Tin Can's wife would like before heading to the big guy's house.

I parked my car and ran inside to grab what I needed. I wanted to make sure I got back on the road as quickly as possible to avoid the evening traffic. Being late never makes for a good impression.

As soon as I paid the cashier and grabbed my bags, I looked up and locked in on one of the most beautiful women on the face of this planet.

Fool Me Thrice

Mercedes.

I stared at her as she walked into the store. *Good thing, I dodged that bullet.*

I met Mercedes at a car wash, and I'm not talking about your average drive-thru spray-n-rinse, either. There was a car wash on Texas Avenue where the women in little damn bikinis wash the cars. It was a brilliant ass idea. The business stayed packed with men, including me. What man doesn't want to see soapy half-naked women bending over, washing cars, and shining tires?

That day Mercedes had on more suds than anything else. She didn't need any extras to get my attention, but as soon as I pulled up, she was the one who caught my eye. When she walked through the rinse cycle, she flushed away all of my restraints. Then she stuck to me like a wet tee shirt. I wanted her, and she needed me.

She needed money. She needed her own car. She needed groceries. She needed rent. She just needed every damn thing. Well, she got all that and then some out of me.

Not only was she a chocolate goddess with a nice ass, firm titties, and a cute little body, but she also had the legs of a runway model. Mercedes was one of many women I was fooling with at the time. But I actually enjoyed having her around.

There was just something about Mercedes. Ironically enough, she had extensive knowledge of cars. Just hearing her talk about luxury rides always turned me on. She even talked me into leasing a Bugatti.

After I drove away from the dealership, she worked my joystick like a NASCAR driver. Mercedes hit every damn gear I had. I came real close to rear-ending and side-swiping everything in my way while Mercedes sucked all my brains out. Hell, I never made it home that day. I simply drove and drove until the car ran empty.

For about two months, Mercedes had my nose wide open. Some would even say she drove a truck right through it. But it soon started to change because of her constant requests for stacks of cash. She was draining me, so I had no choice but to fall back.

As soon as I started slacking on her bills, she announced she was pregnant. Yes, I was screwing her all the time, but we weren't exclusive. I knew it, and she knew it too. Sad to say, but she wasn't lying. She was definitely pregnant. I had my concerns, but I stayed supportive of Mercedes to the very end.

I was young, dumb, and running around with grown-ass women who only saw me as a dollar sign. I wasn't ready to be a daddy, and I didn't hide that from her. However, I also made it very clear that I would do what I had to do if the baby was mine.

I kept in contact throughout her pregnancy. But, I was still traveling the world and being with whoever I wanted to.

When the baby arrived, I flew home so I wouldn't miss the birth. As soon as I saw that kid, I knew he wasn't my son. Mercedes swore it was my son, but it wasn't. The DNA test confirmed my doubts. I never spoke to Mercedes' ass again after that. I guess she was the type my mom was afraid I'd run into.

Just as I started to think about how much I missed my mother, I heard my GPS say, "You have arrived at your destination."

"Holy shit!"

I stared in amazement at the two-story brick house with the three-car garage sitting on about three acres of land. Even with Tin-Can's position, there was no way in hell he could afford all of that with his salary from Houston City Sanitation.

Seeing his place made me flashback to what I used to have. My old house was double the size. Seven bedrooms. Eight bathrooms. It was the house of my mother's dreams. Now, was someone else's good fortune.

The taxes on it were as big as the house mortgage itself. After getting behind for three years due to my lack of responsibility, I lost my family estate.

"Glad you made it," Tin-Can's wife greeted me as she opened the front door. Lately, I had seen her pretty often at the job. She came to have lunch with Tin-Can at least once a week.

"Thanks for having me. I picked some things up for you on the way here. I hope you enjoy them." As soon as she opened the bag, a broad smile spread across her face.

"Oh, thank you so much, Charlie. These cookies are going to great with everything I have planned for dessert." She walked over to me and gave me the biggest hug.

Guess all of them are some damn huggers.

The large chandelier in the foyer caught my attention. It took a moment for me to look away and focus on something else. It was eerily similar to the one that used to hang in my parents' house. I was thoroughly impressed with how Tin-Can's wife had the house decorated like a page out of a magazine. Mom would have begged this lady for tips of her grace and creativity.

"Hey, hey, son," Tin-Can said.

"What's up, man. Wow, your house. Man, oh man!"

"This is where all my damn money goes."

"The job did all this?"

Tin-Can grinned slyly but never answered my question. Tin-Can had three daughters. Two were in high school; one a senior and the other a freshman. He also had another daughter who was around my age or maybe a little older.

The two girls present, Violet and Velvet, greeted me with a giggly smile.

"Did Gabby say if she was going to make it?" Tin-Can asked.

"That's your daughter. You know how she is," Vicki responded right back to him.

"Well, dinner is almost ready. I'll give it another thirty minutes or so." It was obvious Mrs. Vicki was signaling for us to find something else to do in the meantime.

Tin-Can nudged my arm and signaled for me to follow behind him. He ushered me from the kitchen to his huge but gaudy man-cave. It was exactly the impression I had of him.

The room was full of mounted deer heads, stuffed rabbits, and dried out beaver tails. He had a large bar area and an oversized pool table. Of course, there was the painting of dogs playing billiards plastered on the wall. I would be remiss not to mention his large bearskin rug in the center of the floor.

Naturally, I stood next to the bar. It wasn't because I wanted a drink. There just weren't many places to take a seat.

"What will it be?" Tin-Can asked as he opened the fridge.

I didn't want to break my resolve against drinking, but he was trying to build a bond. So, I figured why not. I had proven that I was no good at commitments anyway.

"I'll take a beer."

Tin-Can didn't waste any time asking questions. "So, you didn't have a date to bring? I told you to bring one along. A handsome kid like yourself should have a lady friend. I know you have these women running behind you like they don't have any sense."

I was flattered by Tin-Can's compliments. I'm a tall, dark-skinned guy who has never been more than two-hundred twenty pounds. I always keep a low fade with a nice groom beard to match. I have shapely lips that made me feel somewhat embarrassed. But, women have always seemed to be attracted to my mouth and the things I can do with it.

"Nah, no lady. No women mean no problems," I said, taking a sip of my beer. "Most of them are money-hungry anyway."

Tin-Can poured himself a small glass of the liquor I gave him. "You just haven't found the right one yet. You just need to put some distance between yourself and those gold-digging women."

"I'm not looking."

At one time, I had more women than I knew what to do with. But after I lost everything, they all left my ass. As the saying goes, "Follow the Money." Ha! Afterward, they disappeared just like my dough. I really shouldn't have been surprised. But I was.

"True that. I know you are still trying to find your way, but you'll be back where you need to be in no time. You lost everything. Shit, we all been there. I've been there. So, I know what it feels like. But life goes on. HCS is not a bad place to start over. The company gives out a shit load of bonuses for exemplary work."

"Is that how you got all this?" I asked.

"That…and a few other things from my past. I have some investment returns from the present as well." Tin-Can sat down next to me. "Look, all I'm saying is, I know the income ain't close to the money from the Parlor, but it'll get you to where you're trying to go. Trust me, it will help you feel like a man again."

"Thanks."

"Don't thank me, son. I'm not worried about you at all. You got old Charles Theodore Fuller's blood in you. Your dad was a hard worker and a good man. He helped me in ways I dare not mention. I helped him out a lot too back in the day."

"So, you and my Pops were close?"

"At one point in time. So yes."

I knew most of daddy's close business associates. Through the years, we did burials all over Houston, where I met thousands of people. There were tons of clients who came by the house to settle financial related matters from time to time. Still, I don't ever recall seeing Tin-Can.

"I know you lost everything for now, but your daddy thought ahead. Did he not?"

Hold up…is he talking about my trust fund?

Since I hit rock bottom after coming into too much money too fast, I forgot all about the trust fund. Pops put a little something away for me because he wanted me to wait until I was out of college before I got my hands on any real money. That's why I couldn't cash in on the extra money until I was twenty-two.

Six months from now, I will be hitting that magic age.

Dad used to say, "Once you're out of school, you can use the money on your own to keep the legacy going." Even though he always wanted me to continue the parlor business, he also wanted me to do something of my very own. He told me a real man leaves a legacy behind for his children, and it was my responsibility to figure out what mine would be.

Then Pops told me I would have two million dollars waiting for me after college aligned on the day of my 22nd birthday. That meant the money would be falling into my hands in July of that same year. The big day was happening soon.

I never made it to college. I was enrolled to study business, but once my folks died, I decided not to go. I wish I had. I wish I had followed their vision for me. Maybe my life would be so very different. Nevertheless, in a few months, I would be a millionaire once again.

A part of me was worried, and rightfully so. I spent over three million dollars in three-plus years. So, I was sure my trust money wouldn't last very long unless I did better things with it this time around.

Finally, I asked, "You know about the trust fund?"

Tin-Can smiled. "Yes. As I said, your pops and I were close. I set my kids up with a little something too. We had conversations about this years ago. Your dad and I acted on the idea around the same time."

I knew daddy kept some things to himself, but it would have been awesome to have known Tin-Can before now. I could see dad and Tin-

Can had similar minds. At any rate, I didn't want anyone to know I was coming into some more money.

"We even sought out the same attorney to discuss it," Tin-Can continued.

However, I fired the family lawyer after a dispute we had not long after I inherited everything. If that attorney knew anything about the trust fund, then he didn't bother to tell me. But later, I contacted another representative whose name is on the documents who assured me the money is definitely there waiting for me.

"I was thinking once I received the trust, I could get a late start in college. Now that the family business is gone, I should see what else I was good at. I should just start something of my own."

"Good plan, son. Good plan."

Mrs. Vicki yelled for us to come back to the kitchen. Still, I couldn't help but wonder what else Tin-Can had his hands in.

Maybe working at Houston City Sanitation is his cover. In a way, it's now my cover too.

We headed back upstairs, and my mouth immediately started to water at the sight of the spread.

"Go on and sit down," demanded Mrs. Vicki.

Just as I took a seat, I heard a voice from the kitchen.

"Hello! I'm here! Sorry I'm late."

She walked in wearing a huge smile. Once she noticed me at the table, she came to a complete stop.

"Hey."

"Hey, I'm Gabby."

Fool Me Thrice

Damn!

I was speechless from that point on! Upon seeing this goddess, I lost the rest of my wit and sense of direction.

Art may imitate life, but beauty imitates this woman. Tin-Can's daughter is so damn fine!

***

The dinner and dessert were outstanding, but the night was still young, and I was still craving something sweet. So, I went out to the strip club and came back home with Cinnamon, whose real name was Sarah.

Cinnamon looked strikingly similar to my first exotic dancer, also named Sarah. Sweet Sugar Sarah is what I called her.

I met Sweet Sugar Sarah as I was ordering pastries at a Houston's Doughnut shop. Her skin was smooth like melted chocolate. She had a thing for this unique mocha perfume. She always smelled good enough to eat, and just like sugar, I became addicted.

Sarah was giving me all her sweetness, and in return, I was giving her all my money. I just couldn't resist her. She would smile at me, but it costs me $500. She would rub those soft hands across my face, and that was another $500. She would kiss me with her inviting lips and damn, two stacks. Every time she screwed me, shit…I would just give her my credit card!

But it didn't take long to figure out Sweet Sugar Sarah was a sweet-tooth that had to be extracted. She was creating cavities well beyond repair. Sarah had to be cut out of my diet. If I wasn't spending money, then she couldn't be found. It also became too easy to upset her.

Once, she stood naked in my doorway for about an hour for all of Houston to see. Her knockers, PHAT ass, and bald ass coochie were all on display like a tourist stop in the Lone Star state.

She just perched herself in the entry-way all spread eagle as if she was trying to dry out. She held firm until I gave her a YES to her money demands. But it wasn't just a yes. It was more of a resounding YES! A yes to leave the public view and a yes to pour all of her sweet goodies on me.

However, Sarah always wanted something pointless. She wanted things she didn't even need. It would be a new purse or a new pair of shoes. Sweet Sugar Sarah was just so materialistic. She always wanted to one-up her friends. The only way that was possible was with my finances or with some other fool who had money like me.

Lucky for me, Sweet Sugar Sarah found a replacement because I didn't have what it took to say no.

I kept planning to leave, but Sarah's sugar was far sweeter than my good sense. Sarah ended up trapping her substitute Sugar Daddy with a baby. Trust me, I'm still counting those blessings.

"Ohhh," she moaned.

"Ride Baby Ride!" I commanded Cinnamon, and she did as she was told. I hadn't been with a woman in a minute, so I knew it wasn't going to take long to reach satisfaction.

Cinnamon bounced up and down on me like she was a kangaroo at Charlie Mo's zoo. I'm not a fan of the bounce. I like it passionately, and I like it close. I like the grind. But I had been in a drought. So I took what I could get.

It wasn't long before her mediocre work got the job done. We both panted as she lifted herself off of me.

"Damn, that was good," she said. I watched Cinnamon look for her panties. "That'll be $1000."

"What the hell," I said?

"Oh, you didn't think I came here just to be with you?"

She was a stripper, but damn she should have told me upfront her love had a price. At least she actually came straight, unlike other fake ass gold-diggers.

"You said your shift was over, and after a few drinks…" I started to recount what happened, but she interrupted.

"I asked you if you wanted to get out of there. Yeah, but leaving the club costs money, Charlie Mo."

Suddenly, she got fully dressed in all of two minutes and followed up with, "I take cash, debit, and credit. If you don't have cash, I got CashApp."

Cinnamon placed her hands on her hips and ignored how pissed I appeared to be. *What the hell? All women want from me is money*

Dean Conan

Chapter FOUR

Dean Conan

The next day I arrived to work earlier than normal, but Tin-Can was already seated at his favorite bench having his morning brew. He pushed me for more details about my past. I felt like we had established a bond, and Tin-Can may as well had been my therapist. So, I decided to open up about my history.

I ran through the run-ins with Mercedes and Chardonnay I had over the past couple of days. Tin-Can's big fishy eyes were wide open, his ears locked on my story. Regardless of how much he was listening, there was no way I was telling him about Sweet Sugar Sarah. That would've been telling him way too much too soon.

"So, that's my deal, Mr. Stan. All women want from me is money."

"Charlie Mo, let me tell you about women. Women are unpredictable. They want what they want. Most of them are very smart about it too."

"It's all about money. It seems like every woman I come in contact with only wants money. For damn sure, I didn't expect that."

"Why not?"

"Why not what?"

"Why didn't you expect that? Money is what you show them. It's the first thing they see when looking at you. Why wouldn't they want it?"

Good question. Tin-Can made a good point.

"See, the smart thing is to have money and not look like it. Stack your dough and look broke. Best way to be."

"Is that what you do? 'Cause I ain't crazy. You got something stashed somewhere, old man. I'm sure it ain't coming from HCS."

"I got my hands in a little bit of this and a little bit of that. But that's the point. If you hadn't seen how I was living, you would've never known. Rich is loud. Wealthy is quiet. You are too loud, son. You've always been too loud."

"Shit, I ain't got no money now. But I'm still running into gold-diggers and leeches who think I have some reserves left."

"The more money you show, the more you are going to run into a gold-digger. That $100,000 ride you got is all the noise you need."

That hurt. But my car was one of the only big possessions I was able to keep. My canary yellow Porsche was my graduation gift from my parents. The other three cars were long gone. I sold them once I started going broke in order to pay off debts and taxes I wasn't prepared for. But I can't get rid of Big Bird. That's what I call my whip even though it's small.

"You still look like money, so that's what they see."

I can admit it is kind of crazy to have a $100,000 car and live in a two-bedroom apartment.

"If you're tired of being looked at like a bank, then sell it. Get a new car. Use the extra money to buy a cheap property or something of value. Invest son. Life is all about investments."

Tin-Can threw away his trash and said, "Shit, I'll buy it from you."

"What? You got 100k just sitting in the bank?" I asked.

"First, it ain't worth the 100k your people paid. It's what, three or four years old? Like I said, if you want to sell it. Let me know. Now, come on. It's time to get back to work."

Tin-Can was crazy if he thought I was selling my ride. I barely had six months left of living paycheck to paycheck, and then I'd be rich again. I planned to take some of his advice, though.

When I come into my trust, I ain't telling nobody shit. I'm not giving shit to anybody, either. I'm going to made moves and made them in silence.

Dean Conan

Chapter FIVE

Dean Conan

Going to the gym had always been my stress reliever. Truthfully, it still is. I try to go just about every day. The fellas around me chat it up while I do what I have to do. My whole workout is usually done in thirty minutes flat. And my day at the gym after I had spoken with Tin-Can about my trust was no different.

I wiped my face with my towel and headed towards the exit.

"Charles? Right?"

I looked up and saw Tin-Can's daughter, Gabby.

I found out that night that Gabby was about two years older than I was.

"Yeah."

I couldn't seem to read the look she was giving me.

"I've never seen you here before," she said finally.

"I can say the same."

I would've definitely noticed her. Gabby had ebony brown-skin, a nice round firm ass and sexy lips that were hard to miss. Not to mention her long jet-black natural hair, dreamy eyes, small waist, and big bouncy boobs that would command the attention of anyone. Gabby was impossible for me to overlook; she was flawless.

"My dad seems to like you. He's always wanted a son."

"Oh yeah, Tin-Can is cool."

"I wouldn't say all that. He's okay, though."

"He always seems to be chatting about Charlie Mo. That's you, right? Your nickname?"

"Yes."

Gabby nodded her head. "Well, see you around," she said as she walked away.

"Okay," I mumbled with my eyes glued to Gabby's peach-shaped ass.

***

My evening workout was intense. I barely made it up the stairs to my apartment. That's what happens when you don't skip leg day!

I walked to my refrigerator to grab a bottle of water. It was Thursday night, and I was definitely ready to watch some football. I plopped down on the couch and turned to the pregame show. As soon as I got off of the couch to take a shower, I heard a knock at the door.

What the hell is he doing here?

"Where in the world did you come from? I haven't seen you in forever," I said as I looked at my cousin Ron standing at my front door.

I have some extended family, but as I mentioned, I rarely spoke to them. Even when my parents were alive, we didn't associate with most of our relatives. That's because they all saw us as the bank. They never just checked on us. Instead, they wanted a check. It was always about money.

Once I inherited it all, I continued keeping my family at a distance. But hell, they aren't the reason I ended up broke…I am.

"I moved down the hall. I heard about you living here and decided to come through."

Ron is one of the only cousins I've had some type of relationship with. His mama was mom's youngest sister. Even though my aunt was always asking mom for money like everyone else, Ron was a hustler.

He made his own money and did his own thing. We are around the same age. Of course, his lifestyle and mine didn't mix. So, as we got older, we saw less of each other. But in passing, he's one of the only family members I will stop and speak to on the street.

We dapped each other up, and I moved out the way for him to step into my place.

"Man, I can't believe you lost everything. You know I heard."

"Yeah, Ron. I spent it on fast women, gambling, and everything else. It's all gone. I'm just like everybody else now."

"You were always like everybody else. You just had a little bit of money and a piss poor attitude to go with it."

I noticed Ron looking around my place out of pure curiosity. My apartment was simple and clean. I knew he was looking for the smallest sign of me sitting on a pile of cash, but he wasn't going to find it.

"At the end of the day, we're family. Blood. I'm down the hall. If you need me, just holla."

Ron reached out to me once after my folks died. He didn't get to come to the funeral because he was in jail at the time. But as soon as he got out, he did hit me up.

Ron asked me what I was doing and how I was holding up. He wanted to know how it felt to be a millionaire. The boss. The king. I was in Paris at the time, so I didn't talk for very long, but he said the same thing then. "We're family. If you need me, let me know."

My trust was all screwed up. I felt like everybody wanted something from me. I might have been wrong, but I highly doubted it.

**

Fool Me Thrice

I had been working like a Hebrew slave for the past three months at HSC. My days were long, and I knew that my body needed a break, but there was no way I could afford not to go in with all of the debt I had. However, this particular day, I couldn't seem to get with it. So, I decided to take the day off to relax.

Once I was finally able to force myself out of bed, I cooked some pancakes, eggs, and sausage for breakfast. My mom had taught me how to cook breakfast when I was still young. She said that it was the only meal that you could eat at any time of the day. I would do anything to be able to share one more breakfast with her.

Distracted by the sizzling of the sausage on the stove, I placed all of my food on a plate and took a seat on the couch. I hadn't watched a good movie in a while, so I turned on Netflix to see what new titles they had. Since I was still feeling sluggish, I chose a movie in the Thriller genre to get me going.

After my movie was over, I looked up at the clock and realized I could get my workout in early. It only made sense to beat the evening rush. So, I gathered my things and headed out to the gym.

As I walked down the hallway, I passed by a couple of movers. I assumed that they were there for Ron. But who knows? It seemed like someone was moving in or out every other day.

As soon as I made my way to the bottom of the stairs, I stopped dead in my tracks.

Meghan.

"Charlie Mo?"

"Meghan!"

After three and a half years of partying, traveling the world, gambling, entertaining strippers, and avoiding business at the funeral home, I lost everything: the house, the parlor, the money, and my self-respect. Of course, once the well went dry, the women disappeared too, including my best friend, Meghan.

Desperately, I tried to get back in good graces with my old neighborhood buddy. Meghan had been my best friend when I was just regular old Charlie Mo, but I ruined that relationship too.

She was always around before my parents died. She started at my school during her sophomore year. My parents thought we were sweet on each other. But, no way, Jose! Meghan was a tomgirl who could even beat my ass at the time. She was tall, skinny, four-eyed, and had very little curves. But I would be remiss if I didn't say how nice, beautiful, and smart she was.

Meghan was just like one of the guys. She rarely combed her hair, and she even wore some of my clothes. Yet, there was a time or two I did try to sneak a peek down her pants only to see her Boy Boxers or Granny panties. That was enough to kill my thoughts of wanting to hit that.

We always kept each other company by watching movies, playing video games, and sharing our homework. We had our own inside jokes about how conservative our parents were. Meghan was my best friend for that time of my life.

She was my safe space. She knew about all the girls that wanted me and the ones I thought were hot. Yet, she never appeared to judge me. She was always a good listening ear. No one understood us, but our friendship was solid as gold. She was my Road Dog. But it was well beyond reason not to see Meghan as a love interest.

Fool Me Thrice

Once I got all the money, inexplicably, I lost track of my best friend. I was out chasing the wildest and the most provocative women imaginable. They had pumpkin-sized asses and volleyball-sized boobs. These ladies all turned out to be hybrids (part diva, part fantasy), and I really *really* didn't care until it was far too late.

Foolishly, I stopped answering most of Meghan's phone calls. When I did answer, I took no advice, nor did I try to rekindle our friendship. I was too engulfed with traveling the world with women who were willing to do anything I wanted. Being a Man Ho was my primary focus, and nothing else mattered.

Sadly, Meghan went away. She stopped calling. She stopped checking on me.

I can't even remember when we last talked. It only hit me when she didn't call me on my birthday after a year out of high school. I thought I was the man and surely had enough women around to make me feel that way.

But when I hit rock bottom, Meghan was the first person I thought about. The only person I wanted to talk to. But she wasn't having it.

It had been more than two years since we last talked. Well, she wasn't happy that I reached out for her shoulders, and it showed. The last thing Meghan said to me was, "It's easier for a camel to pass through the eye of a needle than it is for a rich man to enter heaven." Then she hung up on me. I never saw Meghan as the religious type, nor did I have a clue about that shit she spoke of.

Seeing Meghan with a box in her hand pushed me out of the past and made me focus on her. Literally. This lady had ass for days and titties galore. Her walk appeared to go forward and sideways in succession.

Yes, I recognized her face, but she was the whole package. For the first time in a lifetime, I feel intimidated.

"Cousin," I heard Ron say from behind me. "That's my girl, Meghan. Meghan, that's my cousin Charles. But everybody calls him Charlie Mo."

"Cousin?" Meghan asked.

"Yeah. On my mama side," Ron said while noticing how hard we're staring at each other. "What? Don't tell me y'all messed around or something."

I shook my head. "Nah. We were really good friends for a while, though."

"Best friends," Meghan corrected me.

I couldn't respond.

"Yeah. Then this asshole got rich and didn't need me as a friend anymore." Meghan kissed Ron right in front of me. "See you inside," she said as she walked away.

I didn't turn my head when Meghan brushed by me, but I desperately want to. *Meghan is with Ron?* That shit pissed me off. But I tried not to show it.

"Y'all was just friends, right?" Ron questioned.

"Yeah. We were just good friends."

"Cool," he said.

Ron didn't seem too bothered. He headed towards the moving van as I rushed towards my car. *Damn, Meghan looks good!*

Meghan is of a brown complexion like homemade biscuits with a little syrup on the top. The kind someone would overindulge in just because

Fool Me Thrice

they're available. This time she made me totally weak at the knees. She was nowhere near that damn tomgirl I knew. She's only about a 7 out of 10 in the face, but her body is out of this world.

Meghan's strength was always her amazing personality. But *now*, wow! She could be the Bitch of Bitches, and who would care? Not one soul! She was always a good girl. She never ran the streets. She didn't drink or smoke. I don't think that much has changed. But how in God's name did Meghan end up with Ron?

Meghan is the only person I can truly say I trusted, and I messed it up. Of all people, she ended up being with someone in my family. I ain't gonna lie. I didn't like it. I didn't like it at all. So, I sped off as fast as I could. I couldn't wait to get to the gym to work off my frustrations.

"You're back," Gabby said as she walked toward the gym door.

"Yeah."

She stared at me. "Are you okay?"

"Yeah. I'm straight."

"Bullshit."

"What?"

"Bull-shit!"

I held open the gym door as she walked inside.

"How about we leave here for a smoothie or something after our workouts? Then you can tell me all about it."

This time I stared at her.

"My treat," Gabby said as she walked away.

A woman offering to pay for something…? Now, that's a first.

I headed toward the bench so that I could start my workout.

"What's up?" Some of the regulars spoke to me for the first time.

I've never been pressed for friends. I'm an only child, so being alone has never been a bother for me. Growing up with money had been either a good thing or a jealousy thing. So, I'm used to not having too many homeboys around.

But I could always stand to engage in a little gym shit-talking. So I did. Besides, it helped me take my mind off Meghan.

We all introduced ourselves, and I immediately started reading them. Marcus and Roger seemed like cool people, but I wasn't so sure about Chris, though. He seemed a little bit too cocky for my taste.

After an hour of friendly workout competition, it was time for me to roll out. As promised, Gabby was standing by the door, waiting for me.

"Ready to get that smoothie?" She even smiled at me.

"Uhhh…"

"What? Don't tell me my daddy got you scared to talk to me."

"What? No!"

Although I don't want any problems with Tin-Can, he never said his daughter was off-limits.

"Well, come on then. Or, we can turn it into a glass of wine."

"A smoothie is cool," I interjected. I had enough marbles banging between my ears, so I was pumping the brakes. "Where to?" I asked.

"Follow me."

I followed her outside. Then she led the way in her new Lexus to a smoothie joint nearby.

When we got inside, Gabby actually tried to pick up the tab. Of course, I didn't let her. I paid for both of them.

"So, why does my daddy like you so much?"

"I don't know. He's my boss, and I guess he's just fond of me."

"He ain't fond of too many people. So, it gotta be something about you."

"You'll have to ask him about that."

"I will."

I watched her like a lion about to attack his next prey. I watched her eyes. I watched her lips as she sipped from the straw. I watched her every move.

"So, what's on your mind?"

"I'm good."

"You're lying. Woman problems?"

"Nah, I don't have a woman."

"Why?"

"Let's just say I've had my share. Plus, all the women I've come across are the same."

"How?"

"Looking for a handout. Wanting more than they have to give."

"Well, glad I'm not like those women."

"Is that so?"

"Definitely. I got my own money. What I don't have…my daddy does."

"Yeah, Tin-Can definitely has some mad cash flowing in from somewhere. I don't think it's from Houston City Sanitation."

Gabby shrugged. "So, back to this woman that has you walking around looking like you want to fight somebody."

I chuckled. "Really?"

"Yes. Really. You just had this look on your face. What did she do? Or, what did you do to her for her to do something to you? Men are always doing shit."

Her smile had me mesmerized. The sound of her voice was just so soothing. Relaxing. I could listen to her talk all day.

"There's no woman. I'm good."

Gabby studied my face, and then unexpectedly, she giggled.

"No woman, you say? Good." She winked at me. It's obvious she was flirting. At least I think she was.

"Well, since you don't have a girl-friend…"

From there, Gabby asked questions, listened to my thoughts, and answered everything I asked with ease. She made me laugh, and I found myself surprisingly comfortable with her.

Our smoothie date ended with us exchanging phone numbers and her requesting me to call her as soon as I made it home.

No doubt, I did.

Chapter SIX

The following day when I made it in from work, I ran into Meghan. I wanted to walk right by her, but I couldn't. Something about her captivated me and made me stare.

"Stop looking at me like that."

"Like what?"

"Like you wanna take a bite out of me or something."

"What if I do?"

Meghan rolled her eyes. "Don't come at me like that. I was around you for years. You never wanted me. You never made a move. Then once you got all that money, you didn't have time for me at all. So just stop."

"I was young and dumb."

"You're still young and dumb."

"Maybe. But I miss you, Meghan."

"No. You're just broke and got too much time on your hands now."

"No. That's not it."

"Whatever."

"I'm for real. I miss you."

Her face softened instantly. Then Meghan shook her head before stating, "Too bad. So sad. I'm with your cousin now. Remember? Where's that Skank that you're so famous for anyway? Forget it! Bye, Charles."

Meghan left, and the next thing I heard was the apartment door slamming behind her. Seeing Meghan with Ron every day had started to screw with me more than I expected. Even in conversations with Gabby, I still found myself thinking about past talks with Meghan.

Fool Me Thrice

Gabby somewhat reminded me of Meghan, and I wasn't sure if that was a good thing or a bad thing.

***

It was Friday night, and I agreed to meet a few of the fellas from the gym at a local dive bar.

I have to admit talking to Gabby is starting to make me feel a little more human, once again. She was reminding me to live and just let it go. Furthermore, she was entertaining and witty. She asked me questions no one else had asked me in years. Hell, some of them I had never even been asked before in my life. We hadn't told Tin-Can about our interest. We weren't hiding it. We just didn't want to put any pressure or expectations on the situation.

I arrived at the bar in my usual style. My tight blue shirt complimented my dark skin and brown eyes that are exactly like those of my mom. Because of my tall stature, everyone assumes I'm much older than twenty-one.

"What's up, homie?" Marcus approached me with Chris right behind him. They both slapped my hand.

"I'm ready to get my drink on," said Marcus.

We entered the lounge, and the fellas didn't waste any time. However, I was a little more hesitant. It's still too soon for me. So, I tried to limit myself with more responsibility.

Drink after drink, they knocked them back. I tried to be mindful of what I was spending. I had a few months left of surviving off of my checks from HCS. I didn't want to risk being put out of my place before then.

"Cuz!"

My cousin Ron threw his arm around my shoulder while appearing out of nowhere.

"What's up!" he screamed at me, obviously wasted.

"What's up?" I responded back.

"I didn't know this was your type of thing. If I did, I would've invited you to come along with me and my crew," Ron slurred.

"It's all good."

"Oh, baby!" This woman approached Ron, and he immediately kissed her. I had to swallow my anger. *Ron is playing Meghan. She used to look out for me, so maybe I should be looking out for her if nothing else.*

I'm was not surprised by Ron's behavior, but Meghan didn't deserve it.

"Baby, this is my cousin Charlie Mo."

"*The* Charlie Mo? The one who owns the funeral home?"

"Not no more. He lost that shit," Ron answered matter-of-factly for me.

"Damn. Sorry to hear that. You ran around with one of my friends a while back. Anna."

"Anna!" I repeat. "Crazy Ass Anna!" I said again in shock.

Crazy Ass Anna was the sexiest woman I had ever seen. Her body was so perfect it appeared to be manufactured from a mold or hand-sculpted if that was possible. Her sex appeal was powerful, and I stayed aroused whenever she was around.

Fool Me Thrice

She was crazy, though. She was very spiritual and into all the holistic vibes. She also had a thing for personal horoscopes.

She approached me one day and said the words, "Be careful." I asked her what she meant, and she told me she could see the future. She told me I should be careful of "The Snake." Whatever the hell that meant. Then she whispered in my ear, "My genie told me I should screw you like a light bulb." After that, all I could focus on was Anna. Hell, I loved her genie as much as I loved her crazy ass.

I spent thousands on her hunches and premonitions. I was just trying to find the right key to open her legs. After we started having sex, her visions and my future got way the hell out of hand. She started telling me to do some crazy shit I wasn't into.

She once told me to drink a little bit of her piss to bring me good fortune. I knocked that goddamn cup out of her hand.

Another time, she told me having sex with her on her period would bring me good health. I told her I would rather die and would make sure her ass wasn't around if I got sick.

She was just one crazy-ass gold-digger. She followed the stars and the moon. She was always looking for a sign. But somehow, in a strange way, she always managed to make me feel good inside.

She fed my ego with compliments like "You are my Sun and my world revolves around you," or "You are a god from the Old World." Each date was a suspense, and each suspense was a dare.

Crazy Ass Anna and her friends played with Tarot cards and Ouija boards. If that wasn't enough, our dates would end with a séance or a Palm Reading. She was just into it all. For the moment, I had no idea about the doors I had opened. I was lost and following Anna's exotic body.

But finally, I saw her crazy ass intentions.

My money.

She was always asking me to support her wild ass intuitions. The first time I said no, she accused me of not having "The Vision." She said I was being blinded by "The Snake."

So, once my no's became more consistent, she drugged me then rushed me off to a voodoo doctor called Mother Sue. This ended up being Crazy Ass Anna's diabolical scheme to put a spell on me. This way, she could control me and my money.

It all came to an embarrassing end when I found myself naked on the floor, clenching a $50 bill in one hand and hugging a red rooster in the other. Mother Sue was standing over me with her wand while Crazy Ass Anna was frisking my pockets.

No doubt, it was time to dump that diabolical skank. After I made it out of that hut, I made sure to vanish without leaving the slightest detail of my whereabouts. Crazy Ass Anna wasn't ever going to see The Stupid Ass Charlie Mo ever again.

"Yes, she told me you were spending all kinds of cash on her and her spiritual nonsense," Ron's chick said while breaking me out of my trance down Nightmare Lane.

Knowing my image was beyond repair, I didn't bother to respond to that shit.

Next, this girl says, "Baby, I'm horny. I'm ready to go."

Ron smiles at her. "Well, cuz, that's my cue. I'm gonna get on out of here. I'll holla at you later."

Ron dapped me up and was gone in a flash.

Fool Me Thrice

Meghan.

Ron left the bar to be with some other broad while Meghan is home alone.

"Yo, I'm gonna run, too. I got a shorty coming through," I lied to the fellas. I was actually going to see Meghan.

I didn't realize how drunk I was until I took my first step. Apparently, my liquor restraints didn't hold up very well. I'm struggling to stay on my feet, but finally, I manage to make it to the car.

"Damn."

There is no way I'm going to be able to drive. I'm going to have to call a cab or...

My phone started to ring, interrupting my thoughts. Between the dimly lit street and being nowhere near able to pass a breathalyzer, I managed to grab my phone out of my pocket. Gabby was calling me right on time.

"Hey. You busy?" I asked.

"No. Why?"

"Can you come pick me up from Redd's Bar?"

Gabby giggled and said, "I'm on my way."

We had been talking on the phone for a little over two weeks. I liked talking to her. She was interesting. She challenged me.

She'd gone to school to be a chef. I hadn't had the pleasure of tasting any of her cooking, but she had promised to cook for me soon. I could not tell if she was lonely and needed a friend or if she was really feeling me. Her vibe was always neutral, but her body language told a different story.

Oh, and did I tell you that she was a virgin??? I didn't meet too many of them. Gabby said that she was "waiting on the right one." She hadn't met a man worth sleeping with, according to her.

I don't know much about that. I've had enough sex for five men at a young age. Shamelessly, I'm still ready for more.

"Come on with your drunk ass," she said once I rolled down my car window.

"You gonna have to leave your car here until morning."

"Nah, somebody might try to take my shit."

"Your car will be fine," Gabby implored.

A bright-yellow Porsche sitting overnight on this side of town…? Nah, my shit will most definitely be gone in the morning.

Gabby noticed my hesitance.

"Fine," she said.

She disappeared for a moment, and then I watched her get back into her car and place it in a parking spot.

She rushed back towards me.

"I'll leave mine. Now, get out and get in the passenger seat," Gabby ordered.

"I need help with that."

Gabby is tiny compared to me. But she still helped me get to the other side of my car.

"Your big ass needs a bigger car. You got this little ass car and all this body," Gabby complained. "Boy, it's time to let it go."

She slammed the car door close as soon as I was seated.

I liked how she acted so comfortable around me. It was as if she'd known me for years. She really talked a lot about a lot of shit, even without me asking. Gabby loved to talk, and I could listen to her all night long.

"Where's your wallet?" At first, I was shaken by the thought of Gabby being just another money-grabbing gold-digger. But she followed up with, "I need your address."

So, I gave her all of my apartment details.

"Are you sure?"

"Yes."

I think mentioning where I live confused her. She probably thought I resided in a large house like her parents did because of my car.

I was too drunk to hold a conversation, so Gabby gave up on trying to make me talk. She was driving as I toyed around with my thoughts. I looked over at her a little too fast, and she immediately reminded me of this woman named Daisy.

Daisy was supposed to be a one-time thing.

She was the first woman I slept with after my parents' death. Actually, I met her at their funeral. I didn't know it, but Daisy knew my folks from years past. She was in her early thirties, but she looked like she was barely twenty-five.

At first, I couldn't tell she was coming on to me until she made it obvious by touching my package. Daisy hung around until everyone left the house that night. She told me she wanted to make me feel better.

Oh, boy, did she!

After that night, she kept coming around. She kept saying she wanted to help me become the man I was supposed to be. She kept trying to "fix" me, as she called it. When I fell short of her expectations, she would criticize me. I guess, in a way, she was somewhat filling that void my mother used to fill.

She said she was trying to look out for me. She always gave me those long-ass lectures on how I was supposed to treat a lady and how I was supposed to treat her. She would remind me of how the celebrities and big shots went out of their way to spoil her. She pretty much demanded I treat her just the same as those men. But no matter how much I tried to dodge her, Daisy kept showing up. She kept wanting to screw all the time.

Don't get me wrong, the sex was good. But Daisy had this thing for Wesley Snipes. She would call me Wesley during our conversations and even during sex. If I tried to stop her, she would fuss at me to let her finish.

Then she got word my inheritance hit my bank account. That's when Daisy started talking heavily about money. Money, she swore my mama was supposed to give to her. Money, she claimed she was promised. Daisy felt I was supposed to make good on pledges my mama probably never made.

I realized then she wasn't around to help me. She was around to use me. But she wasn't the first person who would try it and for damn sure wouldn't be the last.

"Come on. We're here." Gabby interrupted my thoughts.

She got out of the car and came around to open my door.

"Come on. What number?"

"213."

I forced myself out of the car and made my way up the stairs. After what seemed like forever, we stopped in front of the door, and she struggled to find the right key. After a few minutes, she was finally able to get the door open.

Home.

I wobbled towards the oversized sofa and plopped down with my eyes closed. I heard the front door close, and then I felt my feet lift into the air.

My eyes looked up to find Gabby taking off my shoes. Then she placed them next to the front door.

"Do you need anything?" Gabby asked

I shook my head side to side.

"Okay. Well, my friend is coming to pick me up and take me back to get my car."

I'm not sure why I thought she was going to stay.

"Thank you," I mumbled.

She gave me a big smile and then walked out the door.

I think she likes me. I think I like her too.

Dean Conan

Chapter SEVEN

"**H**ey, son," Tin-Can greeted me.

It was Monday, and I was in a bad mood. I heard Meghan and Ron arguing that morning as I walked past their door. It was 6 a.m., and she was fussing at him for just coming home.

"How are you, old man?"

"Living. Look, we're having a barbeque this weekend. It starts at noon on Saturday and runs until we are out of liquor. I'll see you there, right Charlie Mo?"

I nodded, yes. Gabby had already invited me.

"Tin-Can, I want you to know…," but before I can finish my statement, he chimes in.

"You been talking to my daughter? She told me. Can't say I'm surprised."

"Why?" I asked.

"She's just like her mother. She's attracted to potential. She sees the future in you. Y'all are grown. It ain't my business." With that, Tin-Can walked away.

***

I rushed home after work. I had exactly one hour before I was supposed to meet Gabby at the gym.

"I didn't know if you were in there or not." Meghan surprised me as she stood at the front door of my apartment.

"Meghan, what's up?"

She didn't respond. She just looked at me and stared.

"Nothing…I…" She started to talk but walked away instead.

Swiftly, I reached out and grabbed her by the arm. "You were always there for me. Trust me. I got time to be here for you. What's up?"

Meghan shook her head. "I'm sure you don't want to hear about my problems with your cousin."

"No. I don't. But I will listen if you need me to."

"It's nothing, really," she said.

"What did he do?"

"What hasn't he done? I'm just tired…"

Meghan pulled away from me and rushed back to her room.

"Meghan. Meghan!"

I stood there until I heard her apartment door close.

Ron is out here doing God knows what even with a damn good woman at home. He has the woman of every man's dream. Shit, maybe even the woman of my dreams. No doubt, he's going to screw it up.

After I got myself together, I changed into my gym clothes and dashed off to meet Gabby.

"How was work?" Gabby asked.

"Work."

"Did you bring extra clothes as I told you to?"

I nodded, yes.

Gabby was going to cook for me at her place. She told me I could shower there once we leave the gym.

This would be my first time going to her place, and I was not sure what to expect. She always sent mixed signals, so I decided that I would just let her control the vibe. Whatever she wanted to do was cool with me.

We walked into the sports club together then parted into separate directions. We didn't see each other again until we're walking out of the building.

"Are you ready for me to blow your mind?"

Wait…is she talking about food or sex?

I know Gabby is a virgin, but she sounded like she wanted to give me a piece of something that's never been touched before. For damn sure, I haven't been with a virgin in a long, long, long ass time!

"I'm about to cook you the best meal you've ever tasted."

Oh. She is talking about the food.

We didn't waste any more time. We headed to our cars, and then I followed Gabby to her place.

Gabby owned her house. She was only twenty-three years old and had her own crib. Of course, she was given money from Tin-Can once she graduated high school. Gabby said her house went on the market way below market value, so she hopped on the deal. She decided to go to school locally, which really made it all work out.

We pulled up to a cute two-story white and green house with a picket fence. It reminded me of a dollhouse.

"This is mi casa," she smiled and opened the front door.

Her mama must've decorated Gabby's house too. It had the same aura as Tin-Can's place.

"You like?"

I gave her a smile of approval.

"Okay, so the bathroom is right there. Rags and towels are in the closet. You shower here. I'll shower in my bedroom. Our dinner is already prepped; I just need to cook it."

Gabby pushed me towards the guest bathroom as she headed to her bedroom. It's not until I closed the door that it really hit me.

This is a date. I think.

I wasn't looking for anything serious. At least, I don't think I was. I was just working and trying to keep my head above water. Suddenly, I was reminded of my trust fund. My plans were to just coast until I had enough money to do whatever the hell I want to, once again.

Now, there's…Gabby.

I like her. I like her a lot.

We had crazy chemistry for one another, and her personality was the shit. I just wondered if I would feel the same in a little over five months after those millions hit my bank account.

In the meantime, I couldn't forget the letter from Pops that I found earlier in the day.

Wherever you go. Whatever you do. Make me proud, son. I haven't always been present, but I was always preparing and always setting things up for you to be something and somebody. I know you won't let me down.

It's the most fatherly thing he'd ever said to me, yet it was in a letter. Still, I didn't want to let him down. I wanted to do better this time with the money he left me. I wanted to do better for myself.

"Damn, you smell good."

I complimented Gabby once she came into the living room.

"Sorry I took so long. But thanks," she replied.

Gabby wasn't dressed up for a date. Maybe I was reading it all wrong. She had on a pair of jean shorts and a halter top with her head full of curls tucked into a bun.

"Hungry?"

"Starving!"

She tied an apron around her waist as soon as we entered the kitchen and got to work. We talked and laughed the whole time she cooked. I watched her. I studied her. I fell for every word she said.

"What?" Gabby asked as if she was reading my mind.

"What?" I returned.

"You over there gazing at me like I'm a piece of chocolate cake."

"Damn. I can't look at you?"

She giggled. "I guess you can."

Gabby continued to move around for the next few minutes as I watched her with a smile.

"Okay. Dinner is served, mister."

She sat a plate down in front of me. I didn't even know what to call this dish, but it looked good as hell. I couldn't wait to dig in.

"Taste it."

"Damn, girl! This food is good."

"Thank you."

Gabby fixed her plate and sat on a stool next to me.

Fool Me Thrice

We ate in silence for a while. Neither of us said a word until she finally spoke.

"You're an only child, and you lost your folks. Daddy says you don't have many friends or family. You must feel all alone."

"It is what it is. Is that why you tried to talk to me? Because you thought I need a friend?"

"Yes and no. I thought you were cute too," Gabby added while taking a sip of her wine.

"Oh, you think I'm cute?"

"You alright," she laughed.

"So, why don't you have a man?"

Gabby cleared her throat. "Well, being a virgin ain't easy. It damn sure ain't easy for a man to deal with in a relationship. But I ain't giving it up until I'm ready. Most men aren't willing to wait. So, that's why I don't have a man."

I was surprised I had talked to her as much as I did without sex being the topic of discussion. I've had some teenage relationships where all we did was fool around. I've been having sex (or at least trying to have sex) since I was sixteen

"Well, you're worth the wait," I said to Gabby.

"Boy, stop."

"I'm serious. You cool as hell. Easy to talk to. Sexy as a love song. You're worth it."

Gabby swallowed her drink. "Am I worth a kiss?"

That caught me off guard.

"What?"

"Am I worth a kiss?" Gabby repeated.

She could certainly have a kiss. I would kiss her whole body if she wanted me to.

Slowly, Gabby lowered her lips closer to mine. I let her come most of the way, and then I met her…with a kiss.

Chapter EIGHT

"Hey, cuz, can I crash here tonight? Meghan trippin' and shit. I've been drinking too much to drive to one of my shorties' house."

Ron waited for my response. After a few seconds, I stepped to the side.

"Good looking out, cuz," he said while walking in with a blanket and a pillow.

"She went through my phone and shit. I told her a nosey heifer always gets their feelings hurt. She goes looking for shit just for us to argue."

"Ron, Meghan is a good woman," I said to him.

"I know that. I'm trying to keep her. I'm almost done with my ways. I'll be ready to settle down in a little bit, and she's goin' to be my wife. She just gotta chill out. I'm coming home to her. Ain't nobody goin' take her spot."

But I might take yours. I'm glad Ron can't read my mind.

Kissing Gabby on our dinner date kicked in my desire to have sex. Of course, she didn't allow anything to happen other than touching lips, but she had me ready to knock that ass down. However, I kept thinking about sex with Meghan.

Meghan and I never made a move on each other back in the day. But now, whenever I see her, I have to come inside and rub one out.

Ron made himself comfortable while I went inside my bedroom.

I laid there thinking about sending a nasty text message to Gabby. I wondered what she would say or how she would receive it. But I decided against it. I figured I would just watch a little BBW porn to get myself right and go to sleep.

As soon as I shut my eyes, Ron started snoring.

Oh, hell no.

Then my phone started vibrating.

Who in the hell is this calling my...Gabby.

"Hey, Gabby."

"Hey! What are you doing?"

"Well, I'm currently trying to sleep, but with the way my cousin is snoring out there on the couch, I think sleep is out of the question for tonight."

"Why don't you just come over to my place? You won't have to worry about the snoring," she said with a laugh.

"I wish I could, but I don't feel comfortable leaving with –"

An incoming call interrupted me in midsentence. I didn't recognize the number at all. I told Gabby I had to grab my other line but would call her back as soon as I was finished.

"Hello?"

"Come here."

Meghan.

This was a new number. I guess Meghan saved my digits from the time I'd tried to rekindle our past friendship.

"Come here," she repeated.

"Your man is over here," I forced myself to say.

"Ron?"

"Yeah. He on my couch snoring like a sedated horse."

Meghan was quiet for a while. Then she repeated her request.

"Come here."

I gave it a thought, then finally, I got up and made my way out the front door. This was Meghan, and Ron was dead to the world, so I decided to see her.

As soon as I walked out the front door, I saw Meghan in the hallway waiting for me.

"What's up?" I asked.

She's fully dressed.

She marched toward the stairs and began making her way down. I ran behind her.

"Meghan, what's up?"

She didn't speak until we were standing near my car.

"Do you want me, Charlie Mo?"

"Wow

"Wow! What?" I asked shockingly.

Meghan exhaled. "Do you want me? Like, *want* me? Have you ever thought about us? Sleeping together?" Actually, I had, but I couldn't admit that she was the star of my fantasies.

"Plenty of times," I said to Meghan. *Plus, this might be my damn chance to make this shit a reality!*

"I want you to sleep with me. Tonight. Right now."

"Meghan, you're just upset." I was trying to hold some vestige of being a decent man. Or maybe a decent friend.

"Yes. I am. But I can't say it isn't something I haven't thought about. I used to… Shit, even lately, I have. Upset or not, this is what I want. So, do you want me, Charlie Mo? Because I want you."

My desires started to swell.

"Come on, Charlie Mo. Take me to the hotel down the street."

Begrudgingly, I said, "Meghan, you are with my cousin now. This is crazy, and some might even say nasty, trifflin', dirty, or scandalous."

"So…I loved you first," Meghan added.

Loved me? Did Meghan really love me?

We were close, but she never told me she loved me. I didn't see that coming. My memories of years past are Meghan beating me in a footrace, or Meghan pinning me in an arm-wrestling match. I knew she really cared about me as a friend, but she never said those words to me. No matter how close we were, I never thought of such a thing.

"Come on!" Meghan begged me to get a move on it.

I can't believe this! I've had all sorts of wishful thoughts, but now I'm torn!

Gabby crossed my mind. Shit, Ron being my cousin did too. But I wanted Meghan more than anything else at this moment.

Maybe, I want her because I want to out-do Ron. Maybe, I think I'm protecting Meghan by sleeping with her. Maybe I slept with all those women in my past to avoid thinking about sex with Meghan. How screwed up is that?

Meghan got in my car, and I drove her to the hotel down the street. I paid for the room, and once we were inside, Meghan turned to face me.

"Touch me," she said.

"You might regret this in the morning." I honestly tried to caution Meghan.

"No. I won't. Ron ain't shit. Once I find a job and get on my feet, I'm leaving him."

"But you hate me. At least that's what you said."

"I hate how you played me. You dissed me for all those other broads. I was the one always there for you. But this ain't about that. Not tonight. Not right now. This ain't about love. This ain't about hate. This is about sex. Touch me, Charlie Mo."

Meghan took off her jacket and dropped the spaghetti strap dress she'd been wearing to her feet. She wasn't wearing anything underneath it—absolutely nothing. There were no boy boxers or granny panties to kill my erection.

She walked closer to me and started to caress my face and rub my chest.

"This is long overdue. *We* are long overdue," Meghan chimed.

She kissed my neck, and that's all it took. I grabbed her, and in less than ten seconds, I had her bent over on the bed. I enter her with complete rage and envy. Meghan bellowed out a scream that I'm sure punctured the ceiling of the hotel room. Just as I was about to thrust with full steam ahead, I stopped.

"No."

She isn't just anybody. She is Meghan.

I turned her over and opened her legs.

"If we're going to do this, we might as well do it right," I said before going straight for her nectar.

Fool Me Thrice

This cougar named Clara taught me how to perform oral sex. I was nineteen when she stopped by the parlor to request my services.

Clara's husband had just passed away. She wanted to know if I was as good as my father with beautifying a corpse. I told her I wasn't. This ugly motherfucker would need more than me or my daddy's skills to make him look good.

"Are you sure you want this funeral to be an open casket? You know we do cremations as well," I stated. Clara appeared to be more focused on seducing me than burying her dead husband. So, I told her I wasn't taking any new bodies because I was scheduled to leave town the next day.

Traveling was always my excuse to get out of reconstructing severely damaged bodies. In this case, I would have needed to turn a dog into a prince.

Clara said she would find someone else to prepare her husband for burial, but she continued flirting with me. Without missing another beat, she offered me sex.

She went on and on about how handsome I was. Then she told me she could teach me a few things. At first, I thought she was kidding. She wasn't.

Cougar Clara dropped down to her knees then attempted to rip my pants off. I resisted for as long as I possibly could. I told her she was old enough to be my mother, and her husband had just passed away. I even said, "Ma'am, you're supposed to be grieving."

It didn't matter what I said. It was obvious she lost all respect for her dead husband. She just didn't care. She started talking dirty and telling me all the things she wanted to do to me. I took one last act of restraint by saying, "Mrs. Clara, your husband is lying right over there."

She responded with, "I think his eyes are closed. Why don't you close yours?"

So, I stopped fighting and let her suck me until my eyes nearly popped out of my head. Hands down, she was the best I'd ever had.

I was amazed at how good it felt, and then I realized she had taken her damn teeth out of her mouth. Nothing but gums, tongue, and spit. Surprisingly, it didn't take her long to get me right.

Once she was finished, she told me to do her. I laughed. But she told me she was going to teach me how to do something that would get me any woman I wanted. She told me that knowing how to please a woman with my mouth was worth more than gold.

Then I thought, *shit, what the hell.* So, I learned how to perform oral sex the right way that day.

Meghan's moaning placed my focus back on her coochie. My phone was ringing off the hook, but I was too busy giving Meghan the business. I was busy pleasing the girl that should've been mine.

Meghan squealed as I moved my tongue. With her back arched, she clawed at the covers on the bed. She mumbled my name, and for a split second, I have a thought.

Ron has been screwing Meghan for quite a while and every other chick too. What the hell did I just get my mouth into?

It was too late, though. I was in too deep. But I reminded myself not to go back in Meghan without a condom. I wasn't sure how she was going to take that, but you can never be too careful.

Still, I performed until she started to scream. I knew she was about to lose it, so I licked faster and harder…

Yes! Meghan is done.

She exhaled and motioned for me to take her spot on the bed.

As soon as I laid on my back, Meghan didn't hesitate to return the favor. Slowly, she led my wood to the back of her throat.

Shit, after about ten strokes…

"Damn, my bad."

Meghan laughed. "It's okay. Now that you got that one out the way, you should be good to go."

"Uh, did you bring a condom?" I asked.

Meghan looked at me and said, "No."

"Damn, me neither. We gotta get a condom. No offense, but I ain't trying to make any more mistakes."

I could tell she wanted it all.

My phone started to ring again.

"Let's just go back home. We can finish this some other time."

Meghan agreed. She got out of the bed and slipped on her dress. She didn't say much more while I got myself together. I was somewhat pissed because I spent over $100 on a room we barely used.

"Thank you," Meghan said.

"Thank me?"

"Yes. Thank you, Charlie Mo." Meghan gave a half-smile and hurried inside the apartment building.

A few minutes later, I walked to my room as well.

Back at my place, Ron was still knocked out and still snoring. I made my way to my bedroom and shut the door behind me. Before I laid down, I decided to check my phone.

Gabby had called me four times and left a text as well.

"Was that you who just turned into the hotel?"

Chapter NINE

"Yo, you should've told me I would be painting another man's penis."

Gabby laughed out loud. "Relax. It's just art. You're comfortable with your sexuality…right? I'm pretty sure you watch porn. You've seen a penis or two in your lifetime. Now, pick up your brush."

I agreed to go to a live painting class with Gabby, but I didn't know what I was getting myself into.

The other night she saw me going to the hotel, but I lied and told her it wasn't me. I'm not sure why. We weren't in a relationship. Even though we kissed, we were still just friends. I guess I just didn't want to hurt her feelings.

After we got off the phone, Gabby said she went to pick up a friend who needed a ride. As she was passing by the hotel, she saw me turning into the guest parking lot. Amazingly, after I said it wasn't me, Gabby didn't ask any more questions. Even though I had never seen another yellow Porsche in this area, Gabby accepted my denial

I'm pretty sure she knew it was me. So, either she didn't care what I was doing or figured it was none of her business. And if I'm honest, it wasn't. Unfortunately, I hadn't seen or spoken to Meghan since that night.

Ron was gone before I woke up the next morning. I've only seen him once since his sleepover. He did thank me for letting him crash and promised not to make it a habit. I knew damn well he wouldn't be using my apartment as a refuge. That was his first and last time sleeping at my place.

Furthermore, I didn't feel bad about hooking up with Meghan. Yes, Ron is family but family is more than just blood. Blood is the only thing we share or have in common. Like Meghan said, we had something first. Even if we never acted on it.

"What's on your mind?" Gabby asked while stroking her brush.

"You," I lied.

No doubt, I now had a real desire for Meghan, but Gabby was stealing the show. Gabby was becoming more consistent; she was something new in my life. But in a lot of ways, I was afraid. I tended to lose everything I ended up caring about.

"I don't give a damn what you say, I ain't drawing another man's penis," I said before I started doing my own thing.

After the most uncomfortable hour of my life, we finally decided to leave for some ice cream. We ended up holding hands for the very first time.

"Charlie Mo?"

I looked back.

Damn, that's Meghan!

"Meghan. What's up?"

"Nothing."

Meghan looked over at Gabby.

"Meghan, this is my friend Gabby. Gabby, this is my –friend Meghan. At least we used to be."

The girls smiled at each other, but Meghan's stare is intense.

"Well, I'll let you guys finish your ice cream. Nice seeing you, Charlie Mo." Just like that, Meghan walked away.

"Okay, so how many times have you screwed her?" Gabby laughed as she watched Meghan walk off.

"What?"

"Clearly, you guys have some history, and I'm sure it's more than just old friends."

"We've never had sex," I said. Honestly, that part depends on who you ask, but I wasn't telling Gabby that either.

"Hmmm…Well, she definitely wanted to in case you never knew it. She probably still wants to!" Gabby just wouldn't let up.

It took everything within me not to glance back at Meghan. But hell yeah, I wanted to finish what Meghan and I started.

"Are you free tonight?" Gabby asked, bringing me back to reality.

"Yeah. What's up?"

"Will you come over?"

"Sure. You're cooking?"

Gabby grinned. "You need more than food."

"Say what?"

"I want you."

"I thought you were saving yourself for somebody special."

"I am. You're special. Plus, it's my body, and you are who I want to give it to. Is that a problem?"

"Hell no, it ain't a problem." I was used to gold-diggers putting their shit out there with the quickness but not a classy girl like Gabby. However, there was no way I was going to turn her body down.

Fool Me Thrice

Gabby was a virgin, so I knew her coochie was good and tight.

"Look, I mean, we – "

"We're friends. I'm not asking you to marry me. I'm not asking you to be my boyfriend or commit to me. I'm asking you to make love to me. Well, have sex with me but don't just bang me out. I want it good, nice, and slow. Can you do that?"

"Hell yeah! I can do that. I can do that *real well*. Trust me. You're in good hands."

Suddenly, there was an awkward pause.

"Well, I have a few things to do. See you later?" she added before backing away.

"I'll be there," is all I could manage to say.

Still, everything about Gabby was just easy. Simple. Gabby didn't want anything from me. She didn't judge me. She didn't care about my past. She wasn't asking for anything except to have sex with me. She wasn't trying to force me into something I wasn't ready for. She was... perfect.

I met this woman a few years ago that made me think she was perfect. At least I thought so.

Brenda.

Brenda was easy, just like my Gabby.

She didn't ask me for money. But what she wanted was way more expensive. She wanted my time. She wanted my attention. Plus, Brenda wanted all my Hard Ass Wood all the damn time.

Funny how we met while I was buying condoms. She made a joke about the number of boxes I had in my hand. I certainly had plenty of them too. Due to my search for affection, I was screwing all kinds of women all over the world. Yet, I did try to use protection all the time for the most part. Still, I had a few slip-ups here and there. But after that baby scare, I was more careful than I had ever been.

Brenda got my attention by telling me to save one of the condom boxes for her. After that, she gave me her phone number. I did call, but it was three days later.

Brenda didn't seem bothered by my delay to hook up with her. So, just like Gabby, Brenda and I bonded like we were old friends. But in contrast, Brenda broke me off the very first night and the night after that and the night after that. No doubt, I was clearly the prude in that relationship.

Brenda appeared simple, easy, and perfect. But as soon as I got comfortable, things began to change.

It was all good until Brenda asked me about my past relationships and wondered why I didn't want to settle down. She always wanted me to talk about my feelings. Then Brenda made it known she wanted to take things to the next level.

But I always told her no. I would tell her I was young and enjoying my life. I didn't want to be tied down to her or anyone. I was living the dream, and I had more than enough money and women to kept me entertained.

Once Brenda realized I wasn't going to budge, she stopped pretending to be the perfect girlfriend. Just like all the others, she started trying to cash in. I became her personal ATM. But when my money wasn't enough, the Real Damn Brenda showed up on the scene. It didn't take long for her to admit knowing about my relationship with Chardonnay, "The Wine Lover." Without blinking an eye, Brenda told me, "I know you took care of Chardonnay, her two kids, and her Jailbird boyfriend, so I know you can take care of me and my son."

For starters, I didn't even know she had a child. She hid that so well. Next, I didn't know money was a prerequisite for having sex with her. Last, why did she think I was supposed to shelter her and her son. So, Perfect Brenda ended up getting her ass dropped out of my life.

After that, I never called her again. She never called me either. But Gabby has been consistent. Consistently perfect. Although she wanted me to take her virginity, I could tell she wasn't going to switch up on me. Shit, I could see myself making life changes for Gabby.

Nevertheless, the pressure was on. I knew I had to put on a hell of a performance. I had no choice but to make Gabby's first time her best time. I had to make it one hell of a night to remember.

As soon as I got back in my car, my phone chimed.

It was a text message from Meghan. *"Let's finish what we started...tonight."*

Tonight? No, any night but tonight. My evening is already set with Gabby.

So, I sent Meghan my message. *"I have plans tonight."*

I prepared for a return text, but my phone rang instead.

"Plans with who? Her?" Meghan asked.

"Yes. Dinner," I said, lying through my teeth.

"Well, wouldn't you rather do me than have dinner with her? Ron has to make a run tonight. So, tonight is a perfect time to pick up where we left off. Plus, we'll have the entire night together."

I started to get aroused just thinking about it. Suddenly, I wanted Meghan. She was definitely giving me another chance to have that body.

Meghan was waiting for my response, but I had no idea what to say. Saying yes to Meghan was saying no to Gabby. Gabby was as easy going as they come, but I didn't know how she would react if I canceled on her. So, I wasn't sure how to respond.

"Just let me know," Meghan finally said before hanging up. I couldn't even get another word in.

I raced home with a lot on my mind. I had two options, and I didn't know what I wanted to do.

Shit, honestly, I'm trying to figure out how to do both. I could screw Meghan first and then make my way over to Gabby's house. Sex with Gabby will most likely take a while. It's her first time. So I will have to take things slow and romantically.

Being confused, I ended up chillin' around the house for a while. Once seven o'clock hit, I texted Meghan to see if Ron had left. She said he was gone, so I told her to come on over.

As soon as I heard the knock at my door, I had a grin of excitement all over my face.

I'm about to bang the daylights out of Meghan. I'm going to smash her like Ron should have been doing instead of being in the streets. Because of Ron's foolish neglect, I don't have to think twice about getting with Meghan. But what Ron does in those streets ain't my business. What I'm about to do with Meghan shouldn't be his business either.

I opened the door and was forced to hide my look of surprise. But, I couldn't hide what was roaring below my waist.

Gabby.

She was wearing a black coat that stopped at the knees. Her outfit was conspicuously obvious. This woman definitely wanted the business.

I couldn't wait. Apparently, Gabby couldn't wait either because she smiled and then flashed me right in the doorway. There was nothing but skin and a bare ass underneath that coat.

"Damn and Damn!" I had nothing else to say but "Damn!"

"Damn good? Or damn bad?" Gabby questioned me. I could tell she's nervous.

"Nah. Damn good."

Out of the corner of my eye, I spotted Meghan coming down the hall. I could see her stopping as Gabby walked into my apartment. I glanced down the hall at her. She was clearly confused. For a brief moment, I thought she was going to come towards me, but she didn't. Instead, she turned around and walked away.

I shut the door knowing I had just avoided a sure catastrophe. But now Gabby was standing there completely naked.

"Damn baby," I said while complimenting her once more. I didn't have any doubts Gabby would look good without any clothes. But what's imagined and what's real are two totally different things. Well, she was no illusion.

Gabby inched closer to me. "Now what, Charlie Mo?"

Once she was close enough, I touched her and stared down at her short, brown, sexy self. I could see in her eyes that she trusted me. She trusted me with her body. I can tell she wanted me, but she was still shaking from my touch. So I kissed her to confirm I want her too.

For all of a minute, we kissed, and I rubbed her naked frame. Finally, in one motion, I picked her up as she wrapped her legs around my waist.

Gabby giggled nervously as I carried her off to my bedroom. I placed her on the bed and then grabbed a box of condoms.

"Good. We're going to need that whole box," she said while eyeing the package in my hand.

Oh wow, she wants sex all night long.

For a fleeting moment, I thought of how lucky I was to be with a Virgin that wanted none stop sex with me. I've only been the first to one woman. Well, she wasn't a woman back then. But she was my first, too.

Nadia.

Nadia and I were only sixteen when we had sex. She was a sweet Hispanic girl that went to my school. She wanted me bad like most girls did back then. But Nadia didn't mind showing it. She became my first high school girlfriend. As soon as we were official, she wanted to start having sex.

Our first time was an epic fail. Initially, I tried to make love with my clothes on. I was even content with the dry humps until Nadia made me undress. Obviously, I had no idea what in the hell I was doing. But Nadia didn't mind allowing me to have as much practice as I needed. Every day after school, she wanted me like it was my daily chore. Once I got things figured out, I gave Nadia what she wanted.

Practice does make perfect. By the end of our six-month relationship, I'd had more than enough sex to make me think I was The Man. What an evolution that was.

Fool Me Thrice

Nadia ended up moving away only a month after we broke up, and I never saw her again.

Now, back to Gabby.

I briefly thought about Meghan but that didn't last very long. I couldn't focus on another woman with such a beautiful naked creature right in front of me. So, I told Gabby to lie on her back. She did exactly as she was told.

"Can I taste you?"

If I'm going to be her first, I'm going to give her the royal treatment.

After Gabby nodded, I slowly opened her legs.

"Are you okay?"

"Yes," she said softly.

Good thing she didn't have anything to compare me to, but even if she did, it wouldn't matter. I was about to blow her virgin mind!

Once I got in position with her legs spread apart, I smelled her sweetness all over again. I knew she was going to taste like a banana split with sprinkles.

I sniffed Gabby once more just to put some anticipation in her head. For a few more seconds, I just looked at her as she started to breathe harder and harder. Gabby's anxiety was taking over.

"Relax, dear."

"Okay. I'm trying," she said but barely audible.

At the end of her comment, I proceeded to lick her bald ass little coochie. Gabby hissed instantly. I waited to see if she would do anything else, but she didn't, so I got back to work.

I made sure Gabby's coochie could feel the warmth of my breath. I purposely took my time because I wanted her to enjoy every second and every lick. Now, she started to purr just like a tamed mountain lion.

I stopped right before she reached her climax. I knew this had to be tantalizing, yet I got a different response than expected. Gabby stuttered and asked, "Is it my turn to do you?"

"No. Tonight is all about you," I said.

After kissing her neck and sucking on her breasts, I put on a condom.

"You ready?"

Gabby nodded.

I kissed her as I slowly worked my way inside.

"Ahh," She moaned out in pain.

"Are you okay?"

She nodded again with her eyes closed.

"Hey, look at me," I whispered to Gabby.

She opened her eyes.

I stared at Gabby, and she stared back while I grinded my body into hers. I saw the exact moment her pain turned into something euphoric.

"Ahh," she moaned again in pleasure.

With our bodies locked into place like a wild grapevine, I made love slowly and passionately the way a virgin would have dreamt about her very first time.

Finally, she started to howl and shake. I kissed her as she scratched at my back. Gabby then bit my bottom lip while letting out a scream to confirm she was on the brink of explosion.

"Ahh!"

I was right behind her. Gabby had her first orgasm, and I had one too that's just above satisfactory.

Oh God, yes!

I'm sure I looked like a clown who forgot his routine. Orgasms tended to get me out of sorts; however, round two was going to be so much better.

I stopped and waited for Gabby to say something.

"So, that's what sex is," she said.

"More or less, but it can be better."

"Really? There's something better than that?"

"Yes, there is but don't tell Jesus!"

"That was good," she said with a laugh. "But come on, I want better. Plus, I promise not to tell that guy upstairs." We both laughed, then she immediately added, "Wait, I'm not saying you weren't good. I'm just saying I want more."

"You can get all the sex you want tonight," I said with a chuckle.

Afterward, an all-night love session took place. Gabby was open to everything I wanted to do to her. She tried every position. She still needed practice, but I enjoyed every damn moment I spent with her. No doubt, sex with Gabby was fun. She was rare and very different from any woman I had ever been with.

"What happens with our friendship now," Gabby asked once we finally tapped out.

"I'm not going anywhere."

"I hope not. I really like spending time with you," Gabby added.

"I feel the same way."

Gabby laid in my arms as if I was the only guy she longed for. After I cracked a few more jokes, she finally dozed off. My phone had been off, but I saw that Meghan had texted me as soon as I turned it on.

"Come here."

I didn't respond. I put my phone down, rolled over, and held Gabby instead.

Chapter TEN

"Do you want mashed potatoes?"
"Yes, ma'am," I answered Mrs. Vicki.

"So, are y'all like dating now or something?" Violet asked. This was Tin-Can's second-oldest daughter.

Violet had some unique features or maybe a familiar look. She wasn't as pretty as Gabby or her younger sister, Velvet. But she wasn't ugly either. Violet's look just wasn't as soft as there's. Gabby and velvet had dimples like Mrs. Vicki, whereas Violet's beauty is in her eyes and her jawline.

"Violet!" Mrs. Vicki yelled. "Mind your business."

Both Gabby and I laughed at her sister. I looked over at Tin-Can and found him grinning as well.

"So, are we?" Gabby asked me as she took a bite out of her steak. "Are we dating?"

Since the night we had sex, we had become much closer. We were communicating all day long. If she wasn't at my crib, then I was at hers. She never pressured me for a relationship or for us to be more. Shit, I was the one pushing to see Gabby all the time. Hell, I was the one demanding to be around her and in her presence.

When I wasn't talking to Gabby, I was thinking about her. Honestly, most days, I couldn't wait to see her. Then, there's the sex. Well, let's just say, "It's the shit." She did everything just the way I liked it. She did everything the way I taught her. No doubt, Gabby was definitely a quick study.

"Whatever you want, I'm down," I answered while taking my plate out of Mrs. Vicki's hand.

Fool Me Thrice

I didn't think I wanted to date or be in a relationship, but this was special. Before Gabby, I felt all women were the same. For the most part, all the babes I'd known were looking to get something out of me.

But Gabby was the exact opposite. She never asked for anything. She didn't want or need my money. She had her own. Plus, her daddy's.

"Well, looka' there! You might actually end up being my son after all," Tin-Can said as he clapped his hands.

Wouldn't that be something.

Sunday dinner ended up lasting all day. We all sat down to eat, talk, play cards, and watch movies together. I never had moments like this with my folks. It was rare when we were all in the same room at the same time.

Most of the time, daddy would be the one missing. We did have a few family memories, but not many. But just to see the way Tin-Can and his family were together was… amazing. It was overwhelming but nice to feel like I was a part of something—a part of a family.

"I gotta stay at home tonight," Gabby said. "I have to get some things prepared for work."

"I need to go home too. I need to wash my clothes."

We shared a kiss.

"I'm gonna miss sleeping next to you tonight," Gabby said.

I planted another kiss on Gabby's forehead and told her to call me when she arrives home.

I lived closer to Tin-Can, so I will get to my place first.

I pulled up at my apartment only to see Meghan and Ron getting out of his car.

"What's up, cuz?"

"Not much."

Meghan barely made eye contact.

After standing her up, she hasn't called nor texted me since. I even texted her the following day to tell her I didn't know Gabby was going to show up, but Meghan didn't respond.

We all entered the complex and went our separate ways.

I opened my door and started getting my stuff together. Then Gabby called me about twenty minutes later. We were still on the phone when I got a knock at the door.

I went to answer, and just like that, it was Meghan. She was crying.

"Gabby, let me call you right back. Okay?"

Gabby got off the phone with no questions.

"What's up? What's wrong?"

"I hate him!"

Meghan waited for me to invite her in. So, I did.

"He's gone to see one of his little sluts for the night. I'm sure of it. He told me he had to make a run, but I saw a name pop up on his phone. Some skank named Crystal." Then Meghan plopped down hard on my sofa.

"Okay, leave him," I say.

"I am. I just have to get myself together. I gotta' find a job and get on my feet," Meghan sobbed. "He used to be so nice and sweet. He helped put me through community college once my parents cut me off. When it came time for me to work, he told me I didn't have to because he wanted to take care of me. The first year everything was great. But these past six months…" Meghan stopped talking and wiped her eyes. "I just want to be done with his sorry ass."

Suddenly, it hit me. When I reached out to Meghan months ago, she was already with Ron. I sat next to her.

"If I had my best friend to depend on, I would've never gotten into this mess." Meghan took a shot at me. "You could've told me what type of guy he was from the beginning – since he's your cousin and all."

"Meghan, I barely know the man myself. We're family, but as you know, we weren't around each other like that."

"Yeah. I heard. His people talk shit about your folks. They say your mama married money and changed. Money changes everything, you know."

"My pops didn't have money before he married my mama. He got everything through hard work and years of sacrifice."

Where in the hell did my aunt get that shit!?

"Ron told them you lived here, and you lost everything. They laughed."

Suddenly, I let out a huff. "Let's see if those motherfucking asses are still laughing in a few months."

"What happens in a few months," Meghan asked.

Damn, I didn't mean to say that shit aloud.

I didn't want anyone to know about my trust fund. Tin-Can knew, but he wouldn't say anything.

"Nothing really happens except I'm getting this big promotion at work. I'll be rolling in money once again," I lied.

"Oh. But it won't be like the money you're used to."

"If you say so," I replied.

"But, you also stood me up."

"Like I told you, I didn't mean to. I didn't know Gabby was going to pop up."

"Where is she now?"

"Home."

Meghan wiped her eyes again. I waited to see what she was going to say, but she didn't say anything. Instead, she scooted closer to me.

"If I leave Ron…can we start over? Can we pick up where we left off before you got all that money? We used to be so close. I loved you so much. You were my best friend. Well, you were my only friend. When you started dissing me for all those women, I was hurt." Now Meghan came even closer.

"But after that night at the hotel, I realized I've always wanted to be more than friends. I was just waiting for you to make the first move. But you never did. So, when you called me up after lost time, I was just angry. I felt you were getting all the shit you deserved! I was still holding on to the things you did to me. But seeing you lately has reminded me of what we used to share. Then you finally touched me the way I wanted for so very long. I knew then I never stopped caring for you, Charlie Mo."

Shit.

Just a few weeks ago, Meghan was the one who got away. The woman I wished I had another shot at. But now she was here in front of me. She was basically telling me I could have her if I want her.

But what about Gabby?

Meghan didn't wait for my response. She leaned in to kiss me. Her lips were so soft. I kept telling myself to stop, but I couldn't. Meghan pushed me back and sat on my lap.

"Meghan, look, Gabby and me are…"

She kissed me again.

"I got a man too. Your cousin, remember? But I don't want him. I want you. I know you want me too, Charlie Mo."

I do. Damn, I do.

Meghan pulled her shirt over her head and unsnapped her bra. Then Meghan paused to hear me out.

"No, no! The other night was right. I wanted to do it. I wanted you. It's just…If we gonna do this, it gotta' be done right. I can't hurt Gabby. You gonna have to handle your situation with Ron first." Somehow, I forced myself to put it all out there, but hearing the phone ring and assuming it was Gabby threw my focus off of Meghan's body.

"You're the only woman I've ever trusted besides my mama. Shit, we both know we had a special bond. But, shit just gotta' be done right."

I'm not sure if I meant what I was saying to Meghan. It just sounded like the right thing to say.

Meghan paused, then she kissed me for the third time.

"Shut up and do me, Charlie Mo," she hissed. She rubbed her nipple against my lip.

Feeling helpless, I began to lick and play with her boobs.

WHOO WHOO!

I was powerless to Meghan's sexual desire. Instantly, I found myself going from breast to breast, lips to breast, breast to lips, and lips to belly. I was sucking, licking, and enjoying the moans escaping from Meghan's mouth.

Of course, I wanted to be an honorable man for Gabby, but this was Meghan. This was the woman that blossomed right before my very eyes.

How in God's name did Ron get Meghan?

Just a few hours ago, I committed to Gabby and me dating. But one head just wouldn't agree with the other. Meghan made it so damn hard! So hard that I was not sure if I could even get my pants off to have sex with her.

"I want you to made me feel good," Meghan whined. "Charlie Mo made me feel good."

With Meghan's help, I got those damn jeans off and got to work.

Minutes turn into hours as I gave Meghan as much sex as she wanted and needed. I'll admit that what we were sharing and doing was long overdue. We made love as if we'd been in love for years. I guess in a way, we have. The sex was better than I could have ever imagined.

"Oh shit! You gotta' go." I said to Meghan after reading a text message from Gabby. *I can't go to sleep because I want to be next to you. I'm on my way over. See you in a few.*

"Why," Meghan asked.

"Gabby is coming here!"

Meghan stared at me disappointedly.

"Are you going to have sex with her?"

Shit, after the session we just had, I don't have anything left to give.

"I don't know. You gotta' go."

Meghan huffed but slowly got dressed. Then she asked if I was serious about being with her if she left Ron. Without being sure of what I really wanted, I told Meghan what she wanted to hear to get her out of my apartment.

I checked around the couch and living room to make sure there weren't any signs of Meghan left behind. I flushed the condom and jumped in the shower. It had barely been three minutes since Meghan left my apartment when the doorbell rang.

I finished washing what I could and got out of the shower to head to the door.

"Oh, getting ready for me, huh?" Gabby eyed my naked wet body while I drifted toward the bedroom.

"I texted you."

"I saw it."

"Is it okay that I'm here?"

"Yes," I said, knowing I had a close call.

Gabby sat her overnight bag down while I continued to dry off.

"You didn't tell me your friend lived close by," Gabby stated. "I saw the woman from the ice cream shop out in the hallway. I think Meghan is her name. I didn't know she lived in this complex."

I turned away because I didn't want Gabby to see my look of guilt.

"She spoke to me and said she needed to get in touch with you real soon."

Really, Meghan?

"Oh, yeah. I'll go by her place tomorrow. She probably wants to vent. She's my cousin's girlfriend."

"Your cousin?"

"Yeah. I never mentioned that?"

"No."

"Oh yeah, we were friends for years. She ended up getting with my cousin. They've been together for over a year."

"Oh, okay," Gabby said.

I watched her undress down to her panties and a tank top. Then she crawled into my bed. I finished doing what I needed to do, and then I jumped under the covers beside her.

Gabby snuggled closer to me.

"Ahh, now I'll be able to sleep."

I kissed her forehead, and before long, she's purring softly in my arms.

I definitely enjoyed holding Gabby and smelling the scent of her skin. Such moments like this caused me to break my promise to Meghan.

Honestly, I really did feel something for Meghan *and* Gabby. Sadly, I just couldn't let Meghan go. No, not right then. And I really didn't want to.

Chapter
ELEVEN

"You sure you and Meghan have never messed around?" Ron asks me out of the blue.

Earlier, he invited me out to the bar. I tried to decline, but he made it damn near impossible for me to say no.

"We were just good friends."

Ron took a sip of his beer. "All she does is compare me to you, especially lately. It's Charlie Mo this and Charlie Mo that," he complained.

Actually, Meghan and I just had sex again last night. Two weeks ago, I thought it was going to be a one-time thing. At least, until we figured out our relationships. But every other day, I was there banging Meghan's brains out.

On one hand, I was falling in love with Gabby, but on the other, I was falling in love with Meghan too. The days I wasn't smashing Meghan, I was with Gabby. Shit, sometimes, I screwed both of them on the same day.

"Nah, man. We used to be really close, though."

"Sex buddy close? Friends with benefits? Come on, man. Give it to me straight," Ron demanded.

"No." I denied sleeping with Meghan again. "Just close. Brother and sister close."

"Brother and sister?" Ron chuckled. "Nah, I don't even believe that bullshit!"

Ron ordered another round before saying anything else. "After my side-piece get this abortion, I'm going to propose to Meghan."

Almost instantly, I let out a cough. I was in no way prepared for that.

Fool Me Thrice

"I can't say I'm ready to be faithful, but an engagement will hold Meghan down for a while. Shit, she wants more…I'm going to give her more," Ron added.

I didn't like the way he was treating Meghan. The shit pissed me off, but I wasn't any better. Gabby made me want her every day. I barely wanted to think about life before she came into the picture. And yet, I still craved another woman.

Gabby was definitely all in on this dating thing. Also, Tin-Can and I tended to hang out a lot. He called me all the time, and we normally worked the same crew. He even talked to me about stocks and investments. Plus, I had become a regular at the family Sunday dinners.

It was no longer just me. I was not alone, thanks to Gabby.

"Charlie Mo, I ain't seen you in a while? How have you been, baby?" I hear a voice behind me.

Fannie Lou.

Fannie Lou was from my past right before HCS.

It has been only about a year or less since I've last seen her. She was around when I got word from the IRS about the taxes I owed for the prior two years on the parlor.

She was literally right there when I opened the letter.

I met Fannie Lou two weeks before that day. I brought her home with me one night after stopping at a Soul Food restaurant. I let her stay around since she wasn't exactly begging me for money like all the other babes.

She really wasn't asking for much except for large helpings of crawfish on our weekend getaways. It was so strange she had such a fixation for this Louisiana dish. Mind you, for the sex she was putting down, I kept her supplied with crawfish, boudin, gumbo, and etouffee. My love life was cheap and very filling for that small amount of time.

Plus, she had a man. Well, she said they were on a break. They were going through something, and she was trying to teach him a lesson. At least that's what she told me. He would text Fannie Lou and beg her to respond while she was turning her frustrations into orgasm after orgasm with me. Her anger would bring out hours of raw passion with no limits. I even tried to help with her teachings by saying, "Punish me, hurt me, and teach me better! Make this motherfucker do right!"

She literally stayed hidden at my place for two weeks without going anywhere. During those two weeks, she was riding me and draining me dry. But she was my listening ear as well. She was the first person I told about my money running out. I told her I fucked up everything that was left for me. I fucked up my family's business.

Her only response was, "We all fuck up."

So, when I got the letter from the IRS stating that I owed seven figures in taxes, I paid it. It cleaned out my bank account, and once it did, she left my broke ass. I fucked up by sharing that information with Fannie Lou. I never heard from her again until then.

"How have you been?" Fannie Lou asked while attempting to hug me.

"I'm good. How are you?"

"Married!" She showed me her ring.

"That same dude you were hiding from with me?" I asked.

"Yep. We got married a few months after that. He's good!"

I couldn't resist, so I asked if he'd learned his lesson.

She laughed and responded, "Yeah, his ass is straight now!"

"You really are a good teacher," I told Fannie Lou.

She laughed again, and I couldn't help but glance at her. She still had a nice phat ass.

"Well, good seeing you," she waved.

"You used to hit that?" Ron asked me as she walked away.

"Yeah man."

"Damn," he said while still looking at Fannie Lou's fat butt. "That money had you getting all kinds of dames! Am I right?"

"Plenty."

"But now you gotta shorty?" Ron sipped his drink.

"Yes. I do, cousin."

"Good…" Ron said. "So, stop fucking mine."

Then Ron stood up and dropped a couple of bills on the table. He didn't elaborate on his comment. Nor did he give me the chance to confirm or deny his statement. Ron simply walked away.

Shit.

I instantly texted Meghan. She assured me he didn't know anything. She also said she denied everything. So, I would do the same if the conversation ever came up again.

I changed the subject. I asked Meghan if she wanted to come over for sex once I got home. Meantime, I watched Ron walk out of the bar with another random jump-off.

***

"Son, HCS has an opening for a new position. Do you want to apply?" Tin-Can approached me with another job while we're in the breakroom.

"Nah. It won't be too long before…you know. So, when it kicks in, I'm gonna take your advice and invest some of that money. I will start my own business."

Tin-Can smiled. "Oh yeah? What do you have in mind? Need another investor?" He grinned.

"Well, I've been looking at the numbers on starting a moving company. All I need is a few trucks and a few workers. We can move in and out of both residential and commercial properties. I can hire someone to handle the promotion and advertising. You can get some good trucks from what I've found for much of nothing. The demand for moving companies is pretty good. People and businesses move in and out of different locations all the time."

Tin-Can nodded. "It seems like you've done your research about this, son."

"I have."

"I like it," Tin-Can confirmed. "So, you ain't gonna keep your day job?"

I knew he was going to get back to that.

"Nah, you got it." I patted him on the back. "I'm trying to build something just in case I end up with a wife and kids one day soon – like you."

Tin-Can never asked about Gabby and me. But I could tell he liked us together. Still, he said our business was our business, so he would stay out of it.

I saw a sudden smile on Tin-Can's face, so I turned to see what was causing it. It was Gabby and Mrs. Vicki beaming while holding our lunches. Gabby was always doing random things, but this was the first time she brought me food on the job.

"Hey," she smiled at me while handing me the bag.

"You better stop spoiling me, or you won't be able to get rid of me," I said as I hugged Gabby.

"Good," she replied.

If Gabby wasn't cooking or washing my clothes, then she was picking up needed items from the store. One time, she even picked me up a pack of new briefs and new socks without me asking. Then she told me, "I got these just because of you."

That was different for me. I only had one other woman that wasn't mama or Meghan back in the day that did things here and there for me. She didn't buy me shit, but she did make a few nice gestures. She almost made me believe she wasn't a gold-digger. But she was.

Be-Be.

Mom did all of the shopping in order for her meals to meet her specifications. After her passing, I tried to keep the pantry stocked as best I could. So, I was out retrieving groceries when I met Be-Be. She was so cute and had a voice as squeaky as a mouse. Her skin was the exact color of oatmeal cookie crumbs.

She was so tiny for a woman. So small that I used to call her "Little Be-Be." She was well under five feet tall. From the back, she could easily be mistaken for a student. But once she turned around, she would blind you with that Triple D rack.

Initially, Little Be-Be wasn't my type at all. But she had a mighty bold sex appeal that demanded my attention. Shit, she got it too. She had so much bark and even more bite that came off as cute in the beginning. But in the end, it wasn't.

Little Be-Be had to have been a lab experiment gone all wrong. Yet, an experience I can never forget. Her bad attitude was much too large for such a small frame. It made no damn sense to package all that rage in that Pandora box of a woman. I'm still baffled to this day how such big nasty words came out of Be-Be's doll-sized mouth.

At first, she would come over to have sex then clean the house from top to bottom. I'm talking about my parents' 3000 square foot house. Somehow, Little Be-Be even found time to prepare dinner and wash my clothes.

I used to tell her she was doing way too much, especially since we were just screwing around. I thought this was extreme, but she felt otherwise.

After about six weeks of rocking her body, I started to see her pint canister popping at the lid. She was fun and exciting, but she wanted me for the things I could do for her. It became all so obvious she was little on the outside but big crazy on the inside.

Whenever I pissed her off, she would threaten to cut me so low where I couldn't take a shit afterward. In the same breath, she would turn super emotional and start to cry. A lot of days, she would toggle on and off in a matter of minutes. One minute she would be happy and bashful, then next she was grumpy and green. Her rages just ran amuck like a chicken without a head.

Almost every other day, I swore to leave her, but I never had the will power to do so.

Little Be-Be wasn't the only woman I was fooling around with at the time. She wasn't even my first choice. Nah. But I knew if Little Be-Be was around, my nights would be unique and interesting. She got me into role-playing. This actually made sense because she was often different people in the same body on the same day.

My favorite was her Sexy-Witch routine. At first, I thought, *what the hell is this?* But it was actually fun. She had it all thought out. She played with lubricants and gels, which she used as her love potions. My tool became her broomstick for fast getaways. She was always on some fun shit. Her games were always weird and boy, oh boy, kinky. I liked it until it became too much.

For six weeks, she'd talked me into fixing her car and paying her tuition to hair school. In exchange, I got a few crazy nights with some unforgettable adventures. But Little Be-Be had far more attitude than I could handle.

My last encounter was after Little Be-Be cleaned the house then demanded a check. She said she needed a loan. I told her a loan was something you pay back. I was sure she couldn't repay the $10,000 note, so I wrote her a check for $2,000 instead.

So, she popped a very nasty attitude. She went on and on about how cheap I was, even though I had plenty of money to spare. After six weeks, she said we'd gotten to a place where I should give her whatever she was asking for. Then she started kicking my shit around the house. She even broke mama's favorite vase.

I told her to chill and get the hell out of my house.

She did.

On her way out, she bopped me real hard with her Smurfs umbrella. Then she disappeared before I could say a word. In the meantime, I never saw or heard from that Little Bitty Shit again.

I made sure to cancel that damn check, though.

"I've been thinking about you," Gabby said, snapping me out of my daydream.

"Oh, yeah, what about me?" I asked.

She giggled and then whispered something in my ear.

"Ay, now, y'all stop being nasty," said Tin-Can as he laughed at us.

I glanced over to his wife. She was laughing and staring at us too. Then she said, "You guys are so cute together."

"Together," I repeated.

Are we together?

We never made anything official other than the fact we were dating. But for the most part, I guess we were in a relationship. We used the word dating. But in my mind, she was my girl, and I was proud of it.

Somehow, I was going to cut away and suppress my feelings for Meghan.

She was still calling, texting, and everything else. She still wanted sex whenever she could get it. But she was still with Ron.

I finally ran into him the other day, and I asked him about his comment. Of course, I still denied sleeping with Meghan. Ron said he was drunk, and he was tripping that night. That's what his mouth said. But I'm sure he believed something else. Ron had a gut feeling Meghan and I were sleeping around, so he stayed home a lot more.

Meghan always complained about not being able to see me for sex. But Ron's actions was making it easier for me to keep my focus on Gabby.

I hadn't touched Meghan in more than two weeks. I was hoping things would cool off between us. Most importantly, I hadn't bothered telling Meghan that Ron was planning to propose to her. I wasn't sure how I would feel about it if she said yes.

"How about my place or yours later on," Gabby asked. That suddenly brought my attention back!

"Mine," I said. " Do you have to work?"

"Yes and no. I'm catering an event. But I have everything already prepared. I do have a ton of staffers to help me, so it shouldn't take me very long. After I get things running smoothly, I will come over to your place."

I nodded.

I wanted to do something special for Gabby. While growing up, I didn't see my parents show a lot of outward affection to each other. Yes, I knew they were in love. I knew Pops adored my mom, but he rarely had time to woo her like a queen. I only saw them hug and kiss during the holidays.

So, I don't have much to go by with regards to romance. I never really had any reasons to pamper anyone unless I was buying them things. However, there was this one gold-digger who demanded I show her a little mystique before sex.

Sister Beulah.

Sister Beulah was a Christian on Sunday, a sex fiend on Monday, and everything else in between.

She was the type who was constantly throwing religion in your face, including mine. She told me I was the sinner amongst us, yet she screamed, cursed, and lied at will. She was totally oblivious to her own imperfections and wanton behavior.

This woman could shame the devil with her filth…but her body could raise the dead. Insanely, I put up with her needs, abusiveness, hypocrisy, and blasphemous ways. Sister Beulah was blessed with so much ass I'm sure I was in line with her damnations just for being near her.

If I challenged her faith, she would get me told with the quickness. I would say, "Beulah, you are a lady of the church. You shouldn't speak that way to people and especially to me."

Her response was, "People like you forced me to set my religion down and get a motherfucker corrected. I always pick it back up after I fixed the situation. Don't I?"

Sister Beulah had me so off-kilter I was going to bed hungry and coming to breakfast with a Hard-On.

She was always preaching to me about settling down and becoming a man of God. At that point in time, I'd had my share of failures, greedy women, and disappointments. I tried so many other things, so why not Christianity.

My family was never much for religion. Oh, dad was in church a hell of a lot due to the business, but he was no evangelical man. I got to experience Christianity on the back end, which was the blessing of dead bodies. So, following Beulah into the church was sort of a new beginning for me.

For Sister Beulah, sex had to be more than just a screw.

Fool Me Thrice

I had to romance her. Wine and dine her. Pray with her. After I met all of her criteria, only then would she jump on me like her body was possessed. But Beulah was in a Heathen's Cloth.

Sister Beulah started researching Go-Fund-Me accounts for me to made donations. She would beg me to contribute to so many causes. Then she would say I was a God Send. "To whom much is given, much is required." She pounded and pounded that passage with instant recall.

I funded about five or six of those things, and I came to find out…

They were all registered to Sister Beulah.

She was putting up sad stories and pretending to be these people so she could get money out of me. Yet, I wasn't alone. She had appealed to other bleeding hearts all over the world. Sister Beulah was just a liar and a thief.

But once I met Gabby, I had been watching a ton of online videos with the aim of getting this romance thing down. Hopefully, what I was planned on doing would be enough.

Tin-Can and I finished eating lunch with our women then we went back to work. At the end of the day, I headed out to prep for my night with Gabby. Roses, champagne, candles, chocolate-covered strawberries, and some old school love movies were all part of my plan.

It was Friday, so I was hoping to give her a damn good evening. Then I would get up and make her breakfast in bed the following morning.

Since Gabby always cooked for me, I only hoped my efforts would go over well.

Dean Conan

Chapter TWELVE

I ran around for hours. Finally, I made it home just before Gabby called to say she was on her way.

I moved the couches towards the edge of the walls and placed two large blankets in the center of the floor. I lit the candles and got the TV set for movie night.

I was feeling so confident and full of myself when suddenly I got a knock at the door. Quickly, I opened it, and there she was.

"Hey," Gabby smiled.

I greet her back with, "Hey honey!"

But as soon as we embraced my cousin came screaming towards us.

"You motherfucker!" Ron yelled once he noticed me.

Gabby and I looked at each other as he hurried in our direction with Meghan trailing closely behind him.

"RIDDLE ME THIS! I went all out and bought this girl a $5,000 engagement ring, but she turned down my proposal. Next, she told me she's in love with you!" Ron screamed at the top of his lungs.

I glanced over at Meghan. However, I was too ashamed to look at Gabby.

"Look man, like I told you. We used to be really close, and that's it," I said to Ron as I tried to profess my innocence, but once again, that fell on deaf ears.

"My woman is in love with my cousin," Ron cackled. "But you know what, you can have her little ass. Get your shit and be out my crib before I get back!" Ron yelled at Meghan before storming off.

The three of us watch Ron until he disappeared, and then finally, Gabby spoke.

"Uhhh," she stammered.

I didn't know what to say or do. Both women just stood there looking at me. Gabby slowly stepped inside of my apartment and waited for me to follow her.

"My shit with Ron is over. Your turn!" Meghan sternly said to me while getting straight to the point.

"Excuse me," Gabby said as she stepped back into the hallway.

Meghan ignored Gabby and waited for my response.

This shit is about to end badly. There is no way around it. There is no way out of it.

"Look, I'm sorry you and Ron..."

"Don't play with me, Charlie Mo," Meghan yelled. "You said, if I leave Ron, we could pick up where we left off."

Immediately, I looked at Gabby.

"You said that?" Gabby asked with a soft voice!

"That was before you and I got serious. Before I knew where things were going."

"Oh, really?" Meghan folded her arms over her chest. "You didn't say that when I was bouncing up and down on your ass all last week, did you? Or the week before that. Or the week before that."

So, there it is!

"You told me it would be just us. Now, it can be. Plus, I don't have anywhere else to go. I just blew my shit up for you! For us!"

With my eyes squarely on Gabby, I spoke to Meghan. "I didn't ask you to do that."

Gabby just stared at me. I knew she was hurt. I could see it. Hell, I could feel it.

"I'm going to pack my stuff! Y'all can have your little pow-wow, but I'll be back." Meghan threw her hands in the air and walked away.

"Gabby?"

She held up her hand and said, "I thought we had something."

"We do. I want you," I admitted aloud.

But it isn't the same way I want Meghan.

I really wanted to be with Gabby and make her happy. Yet, I couldn't explain my feelings for Meghan. There was just something about Meghan that had a hold on me.

"Obviously, you don't know what you want," Gabby replied. "I asked you about her. That's the thing. I asked you, and you told me…"

"I swear! At the time, we were just friends. Things just sort of happened. I didn't plan on it. I want you. I want you, Gabby," I reiterated.

"That's another thing…I'm not sure I believe you." With that, Gabby turned her back to me.

"Gabby! Gabby!" Gabby never stopped once she started walking away.

"Bye, Ms. Gabby!" I heard Meghan sarcastically scream out as she came back into the hallway carrying her clothes.

Gabby didn't respond to me or Meghan. She just kept walking until she was out of sight.

Meghan rambled back down the hall towards me.

"Where do you want me to put my stuff?"

Fool Me Thrice

"Meghan…"

"What? It's us again just the way we wanted." Then she entered my apartment as if she lived there all along.

"No. I wasn't sure before. I wasn't sure until just now. But I'm in love with Gabby." I said this as I turned to face Meghan. I couldn't read her facial expression.

"You're in love with her? But I'm still in love with you, Charlie Mo," Meghan expressed in a disappointing tone.

"This is NOT our time," I yelled.

"Wow! Well, you should've said that before I messed up my situation," Meghan yelled back. "I don't have anywhere else to go…so that's your problem now!" She was still carrying her clothes right into my bedroom. It's so obvious that Meghan knows how to lean on me if she really wants something.

∗∗∗

"Hey, son," Tin-Can chimed in my ear.

He's too chipper. Obviously, Gabby didn't tell him what happened.

It had been two days since I'd last seen Gabby. She wouldn't answer my calls. But occasionally, she would reply to my texts. Even while hurting, Gabby was different.

I was expecting her to get upset, then curse and fuss at me, but she hadn't. Her words were calm and dry. That's the crap that was screwing with my head.

"Are you up for some fishing before Sunday's dinner?" Tin-Can asked.

Shit. It was Sunday. I was sure Gabby doesn't want me there. Then, of course, Tin-Can will know something was wrong if I don't go.

"Charlie Mo!" Meghan yelled from the bedroom. Quickly, I hurried off the phone while telling Tin-Can I would meet him at the pier.

Meghan had moved all of her things into my apartment.

She told me if I didn't want her, then it was ok. But I was obligated to let her stay until she got on her feet.

She was even more upset than Gabby.

Meghan was screaming and cursing at me constantly while demanding I figure my own shit out. She said I was wrong for playing with her feelings."

Yet, Meghan told me she meant what she said to Ron about being in love with me. However, I was still conflicted about my feelings for her.

"Can I put some stuff in this closet?"

"Just keep it in the corner. We don't even know what we're doing right now."

Meghan looked at me and pouted. "Charlie Mo, I am here. You got me. What else is there to figure out?"

"Meghan, you already know the answer to that question."

"I know what you told me," Meghan said while rolling her eyes. We have a lot in common. Before you switched up on me, we had one hell of a friendship. Not to mention what we been doing the past three weeks. You wear my name out in bed, but now you don't know who I am!? Wow! I was not sure why you're acting like this. I thought we were on the same page. Tell me the real deal, Charlie Mo. Do you love her more than me?"

"Meghan, what I feel for Gabby was different."

"More?"

"That's the part I don't know."

I knew I couldn't put Meghan out on the street. But I also knew Gabby wasn't going to fool with me if Meghan was living at my crib.

Meghan told me her folks basically cut her off when she started messing around with Ron. They told her Ron was bad news, and he would eventually crush her spirits. Meghan refused to listen. She started screwing around with him anyway.

So Meghan knows her folks wouldn't lend a helping hand just to prove a point.

Then suddenly, Meghan took off her shirt.

"I'm horny, Charlie Mo."

Meghan was completely unbothered by my confused heart.

"Do you want me to make you feel good?" She inches towards me.

I started to back away. I was already highly aroused, but I didn't want Meghan to know it.

"Nah, I gotta' go. I have to be at Sunday dinner."

"Sunday dinner?"

"Yes, with Gabby's folks. Her daddy was also my boss, and obviously, Gabby didn't tell him what happened with us. He was waiting for me."

"Your boss? So, when he finds out what happened with you and his daughter, will he fire you?"

"I hope not."

I still had three and a half months to go before my trust fund was available. I still needed my job at HCS.

So, I told Meghan I would be back later that night then I left out to meet Tin-Can.

I'd only been fishing once in my whole life, and it wasn't with my dad. I went with my uncle, Jim. I was about ten. He was mama's brother. He died about a year later from a sudden heart attack.

I was almost too embarrassed to reveal to Tin-Can I didn't know how to fish. But I was sure he would walk me through it. Tin-Can just loved to talk. He knew it all. So, whether I knew how to fish or not, Tin Can would want to show off his knowledge.

"Man, you're going to burn the hell up out here," Tin-Can chuckled at the sight of me.

I met him at the lake. It was the last month of spring, but it was hot as hell. Still, I wanted to look nice, because I was going to see Gabby at dinner. So, I put on jeans, tennis shoes, and a nice polo shirt.

Tin-Can was wearing gym shorts, an old t-shirt, and sandals. "Get that cooler and come on," he said while carrying another bucket with fishing gear.

After getting settled on the pier, Tin-Can handed me a rod.

"Grab a beer and take a seat."

I did as I was told.

"Your daddy and me used to come out here all the time before we got started in our businesses."

"Really?"

"Yep. This was our favorite spot."

Fool Me Thrice

Finally, I confessed to Tin-Can. "Daddy never took me fishing. Not even once. I did go one time with a family member, but that was it."

"Really? Your Pops loved fishing," Tin-Can told me.

"Not the Pops I knew."

Tin-Can looked at me with pity for just a moment then gave me a quick explanation of how it was done.

"Man, it was right out here when old Theodore told me he wanted to be a mortician. The week before, we found a dead body over in the marsh." Tin-Can pointed into the distance. "Your Pops was fascinated by it. He just stood there studying it while displaying a weird grin. It was some kind of art to him. Then a week later, he told me he was going to start his own funeral parlor. Undoubtedly, he did. It actually paid off too."

"Yeah. Until I lost it all."

"You wouldn't have if he'd taken his eyes off those dead folks and put some time into you every once in a while. He should have taught you what he was taught."

Suddenly, Tin-Can's fishing rod started to move. "Yeah, baby. Come to daddy," he said.

Next, Tin-Can got back on subject by explaining how he was able to make his catch. After placing his fish in his bucket, he continues to tell me more about my dad.

"Your daddy introduced me to my wife."

"Really?"

"Yep."

"What happened? I mean, what happened to your friendship?"

Tin-Can looked at me with a straight face. "Money. Money changes things. Money changes people. Money changes everything."

He didn't have to tell me.

I knew all about that.

With Tin-Can's help, I managed to catch two fish. We talked for what seemed like hours, then finally, our time on the pier came to an end. Moments later, I followed Tin-Can home.

I wasn't sure how Gabby was going to react when she saw me. I could've easily texted to warn her, but I didn't. I wanted to see her face to face. I needed a chance to explain myself.

When we arrived at the house, Gabby's car was already there.

"Here, baby. We did good." Tin-Can greeted his wife while handing her our pail of fish.

"Only two of those are mine. Mr. Stan caught the rest of them," I said to Mrs. Vicki. Then instantly, Gabby turned around at the sound of my voice.

I could tell she didn't know how to respond or what to say. Slowly, I approached her.

"Hey."

Gabby just stared at me. I could also feel all eyes on us.

"I'm mad at you!"

"Uh oh! Trouble in paradise," her sister Velvet sang.

Gabby grabbed my hand and led me outside.

"Why the hell are you here?" she asked as soon as the doors are closed.

Fool Me Thrice

"Tin-Can called me. He wanted to go fishing. But I didn't say anything to him about us. I didn't know what to say."

"Just say you were sleeping with someone else. Say you are torn between two women. Say…"

"I'm not torn. I want you," I confirmed. "Look, in the beginning, I did miss Meghan. We had history. I remembered her friendship and our teen years. Foolishly, we tried to reconnect by having sex. But it only proved our ship had sailed."

Gabby's face cringed with pure disgust.

"What I didn't expect was to fall in love with you. I've never really been in love. Not like this. But you and your love caught me off guard. What I feel for you was more…different than what I feel for Meghan."

Gabby didn't respond.

"I wasn't sure about us. So, I told Meghan we should pick up where we left off as friends. But now I didn't want to."

"Does she know that? Does she know you didn't want to?"

"More or less. She knows how I feel."

"Meghan loves you."

"I know that."

"Do you love her?"

"I don't know. In a way, maybe. But not like I love you."

I have to get used to saying I love Gabby.

I wasn't sure if what I felt for Gabby was love. But it had to be. Or something like it.

"We could've just stayed friends."

"I didn't wanna' just be your friend," I said to Gabby. "Meghan was my friend. She just doesn't have anywhere else to go…"

"Wait…so you allowed her to stay at your apartment?"

"Like I said, she doesn't have anywhere else to go. If it weren't for me and my suggestion, then she would still have a place to stay."

Gabby shook her head.

"Leave." Finally, she screamed, "Leave!"

"Gabby?"

"Just go, Charlie Mo. Just go!"

Gabby screamed at the top of her lungs, so I didn't try to say anything else to her.

Instead, I glanced back at the house only to see Tin-Can standing there in the window looking at us.

I dropped my head and followed the small trail from the backyard to the front of the house. I didn't look back as I got into my car and drove away.

"Dinner over already?" I found Meghan in the kitchen preparing food.

"No. I didn't stay."

She grabbed a plate from the counter and started loading it just for me. Once a fresh piece of chicken came out of the oven, she placed it on a plate along with potato salad and collard greens. Then she pushed it in front of me.

"Damn," I said once I taste the food.

"You like?"

All I could do was nod.

"I saw your papers about your trust fund," Meghan shared.

"What? Why are you going through my stuff?"

"I wasn't trying to. I told you I needed some space. So, I only went inside your drawer just to make room for my underwear. That was when I saw those documents. What are you going to do with those millions? Your birthday isn't too far away, you know."

"I'm not sure just yet," I said.

"What are you going to do about us?" Meghan added.

"I don't know that either."

If Gabby didn't want me anymore, I guess it was not bad to see where things could go with Meghan.

For whatever strange reason, Meghan still seemed interested in me even as I told her how I felt about Gabby. Although Meghan was certain I lied to her, she was still with me.

Well, I do know Meghan. But no…I don't love Meghan. At least, I don't think I do.

Dean Conan

Chapter THIRTEEN

I couldn't keep up with Meghan's spending habits. At least, not on a Houston City Sanitation salary. Meghan was used to dope boy money. Leave-me-alone money. I-am-sleeping-with-someone-else-so-here-you-go money. I didn't have it like that, but clearly, Ron did.

She said something about her nails one day, so I gave her money to get them done. However, I wouldn't give her $300 for a weave.

"I have to look nice for my interview tomorrow," Meghan complained.

"You have nice hair. Fix it up," I told her.

I'd gotten so used to Gabby having her own money and not needing me for shit. It made me uncomfortable to be needed like that once again.

Meghan started pouting because of my reluctance to give her what she asked for.

"Here. I'll give you half. You have to find the other half on your own."

Meghan took the money out of my hand, and then she was gone.

I'll admit, Meghan living here wasn't all that bad.

She wasn't working, but she kept the house clean and food cooked. She even made me breakfast every morning and packed my lunch for work. She said it was the least she could do.

We'd only had sex once since she had been staying with me. Meghan had just come out of the shower and then walked through the house butt-ass naked. One thing led to another, and I just couldn't control myself. But that was the only time. Other than that, she had been looking for a job and trying to get herself together.

Speaking of jobs, I had been walking around on eggshells at work after Gabby told me to leave her folks' house. Tin-Can did ask what was going on between Gabby and me. He said Gabby was strangely silent, but he wanted to respect her by doing the same. I told him maybe there was a reason she didn't want him to know. So, I declined to volunteer anything as well.

Honestly, I just didn't want to tell the truth. I didn't want to tell Tin-Can I messed up and hurt his daughter. Nevertheless, Tin-Can told me he could respect that and hoped we could work things out.

But lately, I could feel him looking at me kind of funny. Our conversations felt forced and awkward at times. Mind you, I did miss the past Sunday dinner.

***

It was 4 p.m. on Wednesday, and I was thinking about Gabby. This was her workout day, so I was sure she was at the gym. I changed out of my work clothes into my gym wear and headed off to the sports club.

I tried working out with some of the fellas while keeping my eye on the front entrance. I watched for Gabby like a hawk, then finally she showed up. She walked in with headphones over her ears and got right on the treadmill.

I quickly finished my workout. I cut my talk short with the guys so I could get to Gabby.

I stood right in front of the machine she was running on. Gabby stopped and stared into my eyes with such fierce intensity. After her blow-up at Tin-Can's house, she hadn't communicated with me at all.

"Move!" Gabby screamed a little too loud. Of course, she was unable to hear herself because of the headphones over her ears.

I didn't budge. I just stood there.

Once Gabby realized I was not going anywhere, she got off the treadmill.

"Gabby, please," I said as she walked away from her machine.

"Please what? Huh? Please what," she asked.

Gabby stormed out of the gym with me on her heels.

"Gabby?"

"What?" she yelled again. I could tell by the look on her face she wanted to cry, but she didn't.

"Look, I know I messed up. You're the first…" I pause.d "The first real thing I've had in a long time. Meghan and I are just friends. Yes. She was staying at my place because she doesn't have anywhere else to go. But that was it. I want you. Shit, I'll stay at your place if you want me to. I've never met a woman like you. I love everything about you." Then I moved closer to Gabby and touched her arm. She flinched.

"I really really love you!" Gabby shook her head.

So, I put it all on the line.

"Tell me you didn't love me. Because I was truly in love with you."

That could be both the truth and a lie. I was not sure. Other than young puppy love, I had never felt this way about anyone. But I was sure what I felt for Gabby had to be the real thing.

"You are in love with me…and sleeping with someone else?" Gabby questioned with disbelief!

I didn't know how to respond, so I didn't say anything.

Yet, I studied her eyes and realized I didn't know how to make this right. I was not really sure I could.

Neither of us spoke for a few moments, and then suddenly, Gabby walked away.

"Maybe I should fuck your shorty the same way you fucked mine," Ron said while rolling up beside me in the parking lot.

Man, this damn cousin had the worst timing. But Gabby got into her car as Ron dropped his bullshit on me.

"I DID NOT SCREW Meghan. Like I said, we were just good friends!" I tried to reply to Ron while keeping an eye on Gabby.

"Man, I didn't want to hear that friend bullshit. She ain't in love with just a friend." Ron had me in a bad spot, and he kept pushing it.

"Dude! We're only friends!"

But Ron smirked and asked, "So where was your little friend now?"

"I wouldn't know," I said.

"Cool. Tell her I got something for her little ass when I see her. I let her off too easily. I spent a lot of bread on her ass, and she thinks she was just gonna walk away from me that easy? Nah…" Ron said as he slowly drove away.

Ron better not lay a goddamn hand on Meghan!

I was so zeroed in on what Ron was saying, I didn't see Gabby drive off.

Damn, Gabby's done with me. At least it appears that way.

But, I was the only one to blame.

I stopped at the mall to buy new sneakers and workout shorts. Next, I went by the grocery store before returning home.

Damn.

As soon as I walk through the door, I notice Meghan's new pretty face and freshly styled hair.

"You like it?" Meghan asked as she spun in a circle.

Her weave was long and wavy, yet it framed her face perfectly. Her make-up was blended to fit her complexion. Her eyebrows were arched, and her lashes were nicely done. She was a totally different Meghan.

"You look beautiful!" Meghan definitely deserved a strong compliment from me.

"Thank you. I got your food almost ready."

"Damn. I wasn't gone that long. You got yourself together *and* cooked?"

"Yep."

Meghan glanced at her phone.

"Ron had been calling me like crazy today."

"Really." This was the only response I could give her. Earlier, Ron had done a hell of a job of cock-blocking me with Gabby and threatening Meghan at the same damn time.

"Yes, I saw him. He told me he should have never let you go."

"Let me go? He doesn't own me," Meghan said in protest.

Meghan opened the oven.

"Lasagna, salad, and garlic bread are on the menu. Now go shower. You stink!"

I did as I was told. Once I was out of the shower, I noticed a text message from Gabby.

Fool Me Thrice

I read it in a hurry.

"Come over."

"Where are you going," Meghan asked. Due to Gabby's message, I was walking fully dressed toward the door. But I could see Meghan had taken the time to set the small wooden table. One candle, two beers, and two plates full of food were waiting.

"I need to make a run."

Meghan looked down at the food and said, "Okay."

After that, Meghan didn't look back at me. Instead, she opened one of the beers and picked up her fork.

Meghan had cooked all of this for me, and I was going to eat it.

Instead of rushing to Gabby, I took a seat at the table.

"I thought you had to go?"

"It can wait."

I took a bite of the lasagna.

"Damn girl. This was good!"

Meghan and I continued talking as we ate our food.

"Do you want me to go?" she asked once we're finished.

"You didn't have to," I said.

"But you don't want me, right?"

"I don't know what I want!" I admitted.

"Okay," was all she said once more.

Dean Conan

Chapter FOURTEEN

One and a half hours after Gabby's message, I finally arrived at her house. I buzzed the doorbell a few times but got no response. After the third ring, Gabby texted me.

"Never mind!"

So, I started knocking on the door.

"Gabby! Open the door. Gabby!"

I knocked harder and harder until finally, she opens the door.

"What's up?"

"Nothing," she growled.

"You asked me to come over. I'm here."

"I changed my mind." Gabby tried to close the door in my face, but I stopped her.

"What?"

"I said nothing. Bye, Charlie Mo."

She tried to close the door again, but this time I pushed my way inside.

"Get out."

"No," I said.

"Get out of my house," Gabby screamed.

I moved closer to her. "No," I said softly.

Gabby was wearing a robe, which I opened ever so gingerly.

"No! Move and get out," she said as I pulled her even closer by her waist.

"No," I said yet again.

"Get off me! Don't touch me!" Gabby yelled, but she didn't attempt to stop me.

"I miss you," I said to her. "I miss you."

"Move," she repeated.

I pulled Gabby completely into my arms. I didn't say anything. I waited to see what Gabby would do next.

We both just stood there in silence. Gradually, I started backing away. But I kicked the front door closed then turned to face Gabby. We were now standing face to face but not for long.

Before Gabby could stop me, I picked her up.

"What are you doing? Put me down," Gabby demanded. But I continued walking over to the couch. "Put me down!"

I did. But I placed Gabby on her back.

"Move. What are you doing?" she asked again.

"I miss you," I reiterated.

"Stop saying that."

"I miss you."

I started to caress Gabby's legs and thighs.

I waited for her to stop me. So, when she didn't, I tugged at her panties underneath her miniature nightgown.

"Charlie Mo."

"I miss you. I was so sorry." I tugged at her panties just a little harder this time and waited for Gabby to lift up her butt. Once she raised the bottom half of her body, I knew right then she wanted me just as much as I wanted her.

Suddenly, Gabby allowed me to take her panties all the way down to her ankles. I tossed them to the floor.

SUCCOTASH!

"She was just my friend. I want you! I want you!" I kept pleading my case anyway.

"Just shut up," Gabby said. She didn't close her legs, so I took it as my opportunity to taste her.

I was Gabby's first. I knew for sure I'd created a monster in the bedroom. But this time, I was using a totally different approach. I was allowing Gabby to push her limits, and in turn, I hoped she would explore new things with me.

I'm not afraid to admit I didn't want anyone else to have Gabby.

Suddenly, she started to moan. She doesn't rub the back of my head like normal. In fact, she didn't touch me at all. She rubbed her breasts instead. I knew right away it was going to be a challenge to get Gabby to let her guards down.

She was tough. It was obvious she had grown up with one hell of a father. But she wasn't the first daddy's girl I'd come across.

Me'Sean.

Me'Sean was a daddy's girl. She was a brat with a concrete personality. She was strong, cocky, and contorted in ways I couldn't believe. But she was ugly as a motherfucker. She was the ugliest woman I'd ever slept with. She didn't have a nice body, either.

Touching her at times sort of felt like touching a brick wall. Yet, she was cool in some ways. Me'Sean was my attempt to try a different type other than the women that drained my pockets. Luckily, I could get

Me'Sean to bend in ways that only a rope could mimic. Other than sex, eventually, she turned out just like the rest.

Me'Sean's father was a police officer. She told her dad about us after our first time in bed. Out of nowhere, Me'Sean signals me to the phone. Without hesitation, I gave her a look of confusion.

We were just screwing each other…what in the hell was there to talk about?

Yet, I spoke to him and immediately regretted it.

He praised his daughter and asked my intentions.

"Sir, my plans with Me'Sean are to make her scream my name in a few different languages."

I said it to him just like that. Needless to say, he didn't like that shit. Me'Sean's dad threatened to put holes in me like Swiss cheese. Then he went on and on about how worthy his daughter was. But in the middle of his speech, I gave the phone back to Me'Sean.

Then I asked if she wanted me to leave after she hung up? She didn't. Just as I promised her dad, I smashed Me'Sean's rock hard Coochie and made her scream my name like a broken record.

However, she and I couldn't be anything more than sex. She wanted a man like her father. She wanted a tough guy, yet a man she could control. Lord only knows the ways she manipulated her dad.

For a while, she exploited me, too.

I gave her money whenever she asked but never too much. Strange, how she always wanted $40 all the damn time.

Me'Sean eventually saw our sexual arrangement as being pointless. So, she called me one day to tell me she didn't want to mess around with me anymore. "So be it," I said.

However, I saw her not too long ago on social media. Someone married her, and they're expecting their first child. I can only pray the baby doesn't look like Me'Sean cement looking ass.

Gabby was so horny with so little patience. She wanted it all, and she wanted it at that very moment.

"I'm sorry," I moaned those words in between smooches.

I could tell by the way Gabby squirmed she was trying to save herself. I could tell she wanted sex in a different sort of way. So, I stopped kissing her, and then she started watching me like a hawk.

Gabby watched me get undressed, and then she watched me place on a condom. She never stopped observing me. But a few moments later, I was right inside of her.

I wanted to take my time. I wanted to please her slowly and apologetically, but Gabby had other plans.

"This is just sex. I didn't need all that," she said. Then she pushed me off, turned around, and got on her knees. She ordered me to enter her from the back. She even told me to "hurry up, Buster."

Damn, I really really messed up this time.

***

"You didn't have long, son," Tin-Can said.

He's still calling me son.

Fool Me Thrice

Days and weeks rolled by, yet Gabby was still as cold as ice. Occasionally, she did answer my texts and phone calls, so I could only assume I was still good with her.

My birthday was about seven weeks away. In just two months, I would be a millionaire again. I wanted to have my life in order by then. I needed to know if it would be Gabby by my side...or Meghan.

Lately, Meghan had been growing on me all over again. Even though I try to keep things as just friends, it was a poor plan for a weak ass man like me. My dilemma started with Meghan still living in my house.

She was still washing my clothes, cooking my food, and giving me more attention than I really deserved. She rubbed my head, massaged my feet, and stroked my beard on my bad days. She sat and listened to me for hours. Whenever I talked about my future, she was there for advice. Meghan had even stopped asking about Gabby.

Meghan had forgiven me for not making a commitment. For whatever reason, Meghan was still around.

On the other hand, it was sad to say, but Gabby barely wanted anything to do with me.

"Have you planned out your business moves? Do you know who you need to contact first?" Tin-Can interrupted.

"I'm working on it, old man. I was working on it. I'll be ready."

"You better be. I was rooting for you," Tin-Can patted me on the shoulder then told me to get back to work.

Tin-Can was a part of my desire to have Gabby in my life. In a way, I felt like I needed him too. As long as I was with his daughter, Tin-Can would always be an added bonus.

I glanced down at my vibrating phone.

Meghan.

"I'm about to go back on the road with my co-workers. What's up?"

"Ron was kicking at the door! He said he wasn't leaving until I come out and talk to him."

Meghan was still living at my place. Ron and I had our differences, but I thought he moved on. It had become crystal clear that out of all of the women Ron slept with, none of them were anything like Meghan. Ron finally realized he was nothing without Meghan, so he desperately wanted her back.

"I'm about to call the police," Meghan said.

"No. I was on my way."

I found Tin-Can and told him I had an emergency. He stared at me in a peculiar kind of way. He knew I didn't have any family. Well, none I really associated with. I could see the concerned look on his face. Still, he allowed me to leave work. So, I raced toward home.

"Man, look at my goddamn door!" I yelled at Ron, who was still kicking and attempting to gain entrance until he heard his name.

"Tell her to come out then!" he snarled.

It was early in the day, and Ron was sloppy drunk.

"Nah, she good," I said to him.

"She ain't motherfucking good unless she was with me," Ron slurred. "I took care of her ass for two damn years! Me! Not you! Now, she needs to bring her ass out here and talk to me!"

Ron could barely stand.

"Come on. Let me help you get home, man." I tried to grab hold of Ron, but he pushed me away.

"Nah, cousin! I want you to send my girl out of your crib. that was what I want you to do."

"Ron, she doesn't want to come out. She was the one who called me and told me you were out here."

"It's your spot. If you tell her to go, then she will come out, and she will come back to me."

"I'm not gonna do that."

"I'm your blood," Ron proclaimed.

I didn't reply.

We stared at each other for a while, and finally, Ron took the first step.

"You couldn't save her little ass forever," he growled and pushed past me. "And who's gonna save your ass?" Ron threatened.

He wobbled down towards his apartment then slammed the door behind him.

Finally, I open my apartment door. Meghan was just standing there.

"He's gone."

"He will be back," she mumbled.

"I won't let him hurt you.

"He won't hurt me." Meghan then walked towards the kitchen sink. "He's angry, but he still loves me. He was begging me. Begging me to take him back. He kept saying he messed up, and he still loves me."

Again, I didn't reply.

"At least someone does," Meghan finished.

"Yo, what are you trying to say?"

"I left Ron because I thought you loved me. But you don't. You love her."

I tried to think about my next words. I still had strong feelings for Gabby. I'll admit that. But she hadn't really talked to me for weeks. She had me looking at things through a different set of eyes. Slowly, my feelings for Gabby started to cool down. Not much. But some. I was definitely more passionate about Meghan these days.

"Since my job search wasn't going as planned, maybe I should just go back to Ron. That way, I'm out of your space. Then maybe that woman will take you back. I am sure my being here is a problem. If that is who you love and want, then I'll just get out of your way."

Feeling shocked, I walked closer to Meghan. I paused as my heart and my head wrestled with each other. I wanted to be careful with my words. Most importantly, I wanted to make sure I meant what I said.

"Meghan, maybe the woman I was supposed to be with was standing right before me. It is possible that the one I was supposed to be with had been you all along."

Chapter FIFTEEN

"Don't be late," Tin-Can demanded before hanging up the phone.

He'd asked me to come over for Sunday dinner.

"Who was that?" Meghan asked me.

"A guy from work."

Which wasn't a lie. I just didn't mention it was Gabby's father.

Meghan and I were...Shit, I didn't really know what we were.

After I told Meghan she might be the one for me, she kicked things into overdrive. I was enjoying her company and the sex. As each day passed, I was thinking of Gabby less and less. I was man enough to say I screwed up, but I wasn't gonna sit around, crying over spilled milk. I had far too much to do.

It was almost time to receive my trust fund. As soon as the money hit my bank account, I wanted to get my business started. I never want to live paycheck to paycheck again.

Since Meghan knew about my trust, I decided to discuss my future plans with her. She wasn't the entrepreneur type, but at least she'll listen to my ideas.

With each passing day, I was reminded why I wanted Meghan back in my life. She had been so important to me for so many years. She was the first person I thought about when my world fell apart.

"I'm meeting up with the fellas in a few, so you don't have to cook today. We're all going out." I said to Meghan. But of course, I was lying.

Nothing was official between Meghan and me. But from the look of things, we were definitely an item. Yet, not too long ago, I'd said the same about Gabby and me.

"I'm off to take a shower."

Tin-Can had refused to take no for an answer, so I was honoring his request for Sunday dinner.

Once I was out of the shower, I texted Gabby to inform her of my plan to attend. Gabby replied that she already knew.

About an hour or so later, I pulled up at Tin-Can's house.

"Hey, son!" Tin-Can opened the door and let me in.

I hadn't been to Sunday dinner in weeks. I couldn't lie. I did miss it. I missed this atmosphere. I missed the conversations, and most definitely, I missed the food.

Meghan could cook, but she couldn't compete with Mrs. Vicki or even Gabby.

Tin-Can put his arms around my neck while we made our way into the kitchen.

"Hey, Charlie Mo. How are you doing, sweetie?" Mrs. Vicki greeted me with a comforting smile.

"I can't complain," I replied by hugging her.

"We've missed you around here," she added.

Tin-Can's other daughters started to giggle but stopped abruptly. I followed their eyes to someone behind me.

Gabby.

"Hey." I spoke to her first.

"Hey."

Gabby looked so damn good, but what was new. Her head was full of curls, and she was wearing more make-up than normal. She had on a burnt orange top that showed off her breasts and some tight jeans that complimented her curves.

I was stunned as she walked closer and hugged me. I hugged her back tightly while inhaling the sweet fragrance of her skin.

"It smells good in here, Mama," Gabby said while pulling away from me. "I'm ready to eat."

So, that was that. We all ate and laughed like old times. What I thought was going to be an awkward evening wasn't so awkward after all. It was all so refreshing.

"I'll walk you out," Gabby said as I head towards the door.

Violet and Velvet started to squeal. Both Tin-Can and Mrs. Vicki were wearing big bright smiles. They agreed I should come back for dinner the following Sunday.

But I was not sure how Gabby would feel about that.

"I had fun today," I confessed.

"Yeah. It was fun," Gabby said softly.

I stopped walking and turned to face her.

"Do you still hate me?"

"I never said I hate you," Gabby said. "I was just upset with you. Maybe even disappointed in you. But I didn't hate you."

"Okay," was all I managed to say.

I touched the side of her face and started to walk away when Gabby grabbed my hand.

"I miss you," she said tenderly. "Maybe we can try again one day. But for now, I just miss my friend."

I stood and talked to Gabby for about an hour. I couldn't help but think I was going to end up in this love triangle – once again.

Shit, I had been trying to see where things might go with Meghan. But Gabby was saying she missed me. Even though I didn't want to admit it, Gabby's comment about missing me changed everything.

Again.

Damn!

After my conversation with Gabby, I drove home in complete silence.

I couldn't think about one of the women without thinking about the other. I tried to think about what my mother would say. I tried to think about the advice she would give.

My mother was seven years older than my father. She wasn't all that old as some would say, yet she most definitely had an old soul. She said it was because of the time she spent growing up around my great-great-grandmother.

But mama always talked about love. She always talked about what it was supposed to be and what it should look like.

"Prince Charles," she would call me. "Love was an action word. You can always tell how much someone loves you by their actions. Love was the most beautiful thing there can be between two people. Love keeps you lifted. Love keeps you going. Love will make you do things you never thought you would.

"Love is always worth it. It is worth the time. It is worth the wait. It is worth the patience. It is worth the experience and most definitely worth the risk. Love just makes you feel good about someone."

Her words played over and over again.

Love is worth the risk.

I asked myself out loud, "Which woman was worth the greatest risk?"

Even though my mind wasn't on the road, I made it home without getting into an accident.

"Ay, yo! Are you Charlie Mo?"

I looked behind me as I shut my car door. But before I could respond, I felt a blow to the head. Four. Five. Maybe six blows. I couldn't count them, but I felt them as I struggled to stay on my feet. It was just incredibly hard to defend myself.

The lick to the right side of my face was what took me down to my knees. Next, the bottom of their shoes got to work on me. I tried getting back up, and then I realized I couldn't, so I protected my head.

I'd only been in two fistfights my entire life. One time in school, those prep boys tried to kick my ass like it was some type of initiation. I was surprised when they jumped me even then.

It was three versus one. They tried, but I got the best of them. I earned some mad respect after that. From then on, I was getting a helluva lot of attention from the schoolgirls too. Hell, even those fools' skanks wanted me.

The second time was on the streets. Since my folks had money, a couple of thugs thought they could bully me around. Nah, not me. Not Charlie Mo.

A dude called Hammerhead tried to take my shoes off my feet. I had no choice but to stand my ground. A lot of people surrounded us just to see us fight. Almost everyone was cheering for Hammerhead. They wanted him to beat the rich kid's ass. Most of those assholes felt I needed to be turned down a notch.

Too bad.

I beat the shit out of that fool, too. Yeah, he broke my nose, but that was it. After that day, every time Hammerhead saw me, he gave me a nod of respect.

Suddenly, the stomping comes to an abrupt end. That was when I heard the sirens followed by shoes hitting the pavement as the guys ran away.

"Sir, are you alright?"

My vision was blurred in my left eye, and I could barely open the right one.

"Do you know those guys?"

Next, I felt the officer pulled at my arm.

"Ahhhh!"

Shit! I think it might be broken.

I didn't know who those guys are, but I had a pretty good idea who sent them my way.

Ron.

I gave the officer my apartment information then asked him to get Meghan while we waited for the ambulance.

Meghan panicked once she saw me.

"Charlie Mo! Oh my God! Who did this to you?" She asked the questions, but I could tell by the look on her face she already knew the answers.

I could also see the damage to my car through my blurriness. The back window had been shattered. Plus, the side of my car had a dent from the foot-stomping. It was gonna cost me a fortune to get that shit fixed.

***

"My dad told me what happened," Gabby said, sitting down in a chair that looked highly uncomfortable.

I had to call Tin-Can and tell him I wouldn't be able to make it to work. I had a few broken ribs, a fractured arm, a broken jaw, a bruised knee, and a concussion. I was really messed up.

I was so pissed off I couldn't wait to see Ron. We used to play fight when we were younger. He couldn't fight then, and I was sure he still couldn't fight. Ron wasn't shit without his boys, but he was going to see me. He was going to answer to me. He was going to *feel* me too.

Meghan kept eying Gabby while I lay in my hospital bed. Then she looked at me. It was completely silent until Gabby started with her questions.

"Who did this to you?"

I couldn't really talk, so I shrugged my shoulders.

"If I had invited you over last night, this wouldn't have happened," Gabby said.

"Wait, he was with you, again?" Meghan asked after being surprised.

Gabby looked over at Meghan then said, "My father expects Charlie Mo at our Sunday's family dinners." I could tell by Gabby's indignant tone she was trying to get back at Meghan.

"You told me that you were going out with the fellas from work." Meghan shook her head and started to stand up.

I tried to motion for Meghan to sit back down, but she grabbed her purse anyway.

"Don't worry, I'll be back," Meghan said with an attitude. "But Charlie Mo, you're going to have to make a choice. You gonna have to make one real damn soon."

Meghan stormed out of the hospital room.

I exhaled loudly, and then Gabby started up again.

"Wait, so you and she..."

I held up a finger as I motioned for Gabby to get my phone. After she gave it to me, I used my good arm to text her.

She responded aloud to my messages.

"Since things were messed up with me, you decided to get closer to Meghan? You were trying to get back to what y'all had in the past?"

I answered her question through a text message.

"*Basically, yes,*" I typed back to her.

"So, what does that mean? During our talk last night, I thought..." Gabby replied in confusion.

I held up a finger and texted her something else.

"*You do mean everything to me. But honestly, I have feelings for you and Meghan. I felt you would never forgive me.*"

Gabby read aloud what I had sent her. I nodded confirmed what she had read. There was no point in me lying anymore. In a way, I wished

I could go back to the days when I was all alone. Things were a lot simpler then.

Gabby looked uncomfortable. I could tell she was trying to figure out what to say next.

"Charlie Mo, I meant what I said. I miss you. I don't think I was quite ready right now, but I hope we can try again one day. Yes, there has to be a choice made very soon."

The real question was… How?

Chapter
SIXTEEN

Six days later...

"Damn cuz, what happened to you?" Ron asked as Meghan helped me towards my apartment. "Hey baby," he chimed to Meghan.

I stopped and turned around to face him.

"You sent your boys to jump me," I mumbled.

They kept me in the hospital for almost a week. I was still sore and bruised. My mouth still hurt when I talked, but that didn't stop me. "Where are your boys now, huh?"

I attempted to stand. I was still messed up, but I was prepared to swing on Ron.

"What? Yo, I didn't send nobody to do shit to you! What the hell? I didn't need nobody to fight my battles. If I wanted to rock your shit, I would have done it myself. Get the hell out of here, man!" Ron seemed insulted.

"So, you telling me you didn't do this?"

"Over her?" Ron asked. I nodded while looking at Meghan.

"Hell, nah! Oh, I'm gonna get her back. I ain't even worried about that. Like I said, if I wanted to send you a message, I would've done it myself. Trust me, cuz. Had it been me, then you wouldn't be standing here talking right now! You feel me?" Ron growled. "I guess you got more enemies than me, Charlie Mo," Ron said as he started to back away. "Bye, baby," he shouted while turning toward Meghan.

Meghan didn't respond.

"Shit, you think he telling the truth?" I asked Meghan as she put her arm back around my waist.

"Actually, now that I've heard him say it...I do. Ron gotta' lot of pride. He had a big ass ego. He thinks he's untouchable. When Ron does shit, he wants you to know it was him."

Meghan opened the door to the apartment.

"Shit, if it wasn't Ron seeking revenge, then who in the hell wants to send me a message?"

Meghan shrugged after making sure I was comfortable on the couch.

"Shit, you never know who can be out there plotting against you. With your history, Charlie Mo, I am sure there's someone with an ax to grind. Who really knows?" Meghan said.

Nah, ain't nobody got nothing against me. I ain't buying it. Ron did this shit. He's the only one with a chip on his shoulder because Meghan wants me and not him.

"Do you want me to fix you something to eat?" Meghan asked.

I shook my head, no.

"Actually...Gabby said she prepped a lot of meals for me, which should last the entire week. She promised to drop them off real soon. I didn't want her food to go to waste."

I wanted to be as honest as possible going forward, so I forced myself to share this information with Meghan.

"But I do want you to come and sit under your sexy man," I smirked with my raggedy smile. Meghan started to smile back. "Look, I've been enjoying these past few weeks with you. It felt like the good old days. Gabby and I decided to be just friends. Baby, that was all we are, okay?"

Meghan nodded and said, "Okay."

"You and I are old friends. You were always my first best friend. I don't know for sure where this will lead, but I wouldn't try to play you. I care too much about you."

Meghan kissed me and broadened her smile.

We talked about a lot of random things. A few minutes later, there was a knock at the door. Meghan went to open it, and in walked Gabby carrying a very large box.

"There's a lot of food in here," Gabby said while placing the meals on the counter. "I just finished making some of it about an hour ago."

Meghan quietly disappearED down the hall, but I could still hear the bedroom door being closed.

Gabby walked over to me.

"How are you feeling?"

"Like shit," I answered honestly.

"Do you need anything else?"

I shook my head with a smile. "Nah, I'm good."

Gabby lingered for a second, then took a seat while saying, "I would offer to stay but…"

She stopped talking and waited for me to interject. But I couldn't find it in me to say anything. So, I just looked at her. I noticed for the first time that some of the faces Gabby made remind me of Tin-Can.

"I guess you have her, so you don't need me here."

"Stop."

"What?"

"Stop," I repeated. "Thanks for the food. I really appreciate it."

Gabby stood up to leave and then added, "You're welcome. Let me know if you need anything, I guess!"

"I will."

"Alright, well, I'll talk to you later." Then Gabby headed towards the door.

"No. Call me when you made it home. I'll be waiting."

Gabby smiled. "Okay."

Once the front door closed, Meghan immediately came out of the bedroom. I figured she was going to say something smart, but she didn't.

"What?" I asked in anticipation as Meghan stood in front of me.

"Nothing."

Meghan headed to the counter and looked inside the big box. She took each container and stacked them inside the refrigerator and then walked back over to me.

"What?" I asked once again as she stares at me.

"Nothing," Meghan said as she proceeded to get down on her knees.

"What are you doing?" I asked as Meghan tugged at the string on my gym shorts.

Then she pulled at my shorts until finally, Meghan had my briefs down below my knees.

No doubt, I was hard. I was so hard a cat could scratch my tool, and I wouldn't even know it.

I kept trying to stop her. "What are you doing?"

Meghan still didn't say a word. Instead, she started working my swollen tool like a woodpecker.

I closed my eyes. Shit! I was in pain, but it did feel good.

Just as Meghan got into a groove, my phone started ringing.

Gabby.

I tapped at Meghan's head before picking up my phone, but Meghan ignored me. Instead, she kept bobbing up and down as if she was pumping a shot-gun.

The phone continued to ring. I knew I had to answer it. I wanted to get back in Gabby's good graces, but not taking her call could be a setback. I really needed to answer my mobile! So, I figured I could reply really quickly and then hang the damn thing up.

"Hello," I forced myself to say.

"I made it," she said.

"Okay," was the only other word I was capable of saying.

I squeezed my one good eye shut.

Meghan continued to caress and tea-bag me. I was on the verge of saying my "ABC's," but I continued to fight that urge so valiantly. I was sure I had the most stupid look on my face.

"What are you doing?" Gabby asked.

"Still sitting on the couch," I said. At least it was not a lie.

"Oh. Have you eaten yet?"

"No," I mumbled. But I wanted to throw the phone down so I could grab a handful of Meghan's hair. Then I could really enjoy this moment!

"When are you going to eat?" Gabby asked.

"In a minute. Um! Let me try to get up and use the bathroom and call you back. Then you can tell me which container to try first."

"Okay," Gabby said. *Thank God that conversation was over.*

Immediately, I dropped the phone. But it didn't matter. I had no more self-control, anyway!

"Oh shit," I moaned and locked onto Meghan's hair.

"What have I done to deserve this?" I managed to get that much out of my tattered mouth. Still, I got no response.

Meghan chuckled and continued milking me out like a maid on a dairy cow. Finally, I relaxed and enjoyed the feeling.

A few minutes later, I tapped to notify Meghan the well was completely dry. There wasn't even a corner left in that bottle. I was in desperate need of a time-out.

Meghan didn't move, though. Instead, I had to force myself up with the little energy I had left. Dazed and relieved, I struggled to the bathroom

At last, Meghan got up and walked away. She was gone for about ten minutes. So, I got myself together as best I could considering my set of injuries.

When I stepped out of the bathroom, Meghan had prepared the couch with blankets and a pillow. She even warmed up one of Gabby's meals. The T.V. was on my favorite sports channel, and the remote was on the end table.

"There. All set. Now, you can call that skank back," Meghan said and smirked at me. Right before I took a seat on the couch, she added,

"Charlie Mo, you know I know a gold-digger when I see one." Admittedly, I was somewhat stunned. But after that, Meghan headed back into the bathroom.

This is going to be interesting.

***

"Nice to see you, son," Tin-Can said.

Two weeks after being jumped, I was back at work. I was almost certain I'd come back too soon because my arm was still messed up, and my side was sore. I still didn't know who attacked me. I concluded Ron had to be lying. I never had any problems with anyone.

"I heard you were messed up. Son, do you need some fighting lessons," Tin-Can chuckled.

"Look, man, it was six of them. At least, I think. I did what I could," I said in my defense to Tin-Can.

"Those punks need to be put in jail. But you don't know who or why?"

"Nah."

Tin-Can sat down with me at one of the round tables.

"I hear you got a new woman," Tin-Can said. He really caught me off guard.

"What?"

"Gabby told me you have some woman living in your house."

"It's only a friend. We are not together. This lady just got out of a bad relationship with my cousin," I explained.

"Gabby thinks it was more than a friendship. That was what she told me the other day. I was surprised. She was normally so private, just like her mother. But she wanted my opinion," said Tin-Can.

"I talk to Meghan when Gabby is around. I am just friends with both of them. Gabby and I want more, but right now, we are only friends as well. Meghan used to be my next-door neighbor back in high school. She was practically family to me."

Tin-Can nodded. "You kids do things so differently than what we did back in my day. I did tell Gabby I would speak to you about it. So, this was me mentioning it." Afterward, Tin-Can shrugged his shoulders. "Now, about this car..."

Dean Conan

Chapter SEVENTEEN

My first day back at work was long and painful. I was still not myself, but Gabby insisted I try to get my body back to normal. So we scheduled to meet each other at the gym.

"How was work," Gabby asked as soon as she saw me.

I hugged her and said, "It was slow and painful."

Gently, I stood and held Gabby for a while. "How was your day?"

"Long," she said.

We walked into the gym together.

Instead of separating like we used to, we got on treadmills that were right next to each. This was the first test for my sore knee. Nope! It was not ready.

I gave up on the treadmill and went to lift weights. I started chatting with the guys until Gabby completed her workout.

"I guess it'll be a while before your body was fully back to normal," Gabby concluded as we leave the gym.

"Yeah."

Suddenly, there's an awkward pause.

"Do you think your body is up for sex?" Gabby's question surprised me!

I know it is. I was hobbling around, but I am still horny.

But I had to redirect the conversation. I need to knew where things stood with Tin-Can.

"Uh...your pops..."

"Yeah. I just wanted some advice," Gabby said. "I rarely tell daddy anything about us, but I wanted to know if he thought I was wasting my time."

"Do you feel like you're wasting your time?"

"Honestly, I didn't know," Gabby responded.

We reached her car.

"I heard you that night," she continued.

"What night?" I asked.

"The first night you were home from the hospital. Remember, you told me to call you after I got home. I did, and I heard you and Meghan."

Holy Shit!

"You said you would call me back once you left the bathroom. But apparently, you failed to hang up the phone. From your moans and grunts, your friend was all over you. Right? I hate to say this, but it sounded like you were taking a real ass beating."

"What?" I asked.

"Yeah. All I heard was damn, shit, oh God, hey, whoo-hoo, ah-ha, wait, please, whoa, Lord-Oh-Lord, Jesus, fuck, woo, and Lordy Lordy! You don't sound that way when you have sex with me, Charlie Mo."

Damn! Damn!! Damn!!! I thought I hung up that damn phone. Why in the hell didn't she say something before?

"Right?"

I exhaled. "Ok, Gabby. You're right."

Gabby nodded. "I guess friends have sex these days. We're friends, right?"

I tried to figure out where she was going with the conversation.

"Friends have sex sometimes too. At least you do with your friend, Meghan."

"Gabby..."

"I'm just asking if you are up for sex. If so...my place or yours?"

"Yours," I said to her.

I followed Gabby home. Before we even made it inside, she was all over me. She was as horny as a toad frog. A big part of me was surprised she still wanted to mess with me. I certainly had more than a fool's share of train wrecks for her to deal with.

"Do you need help," Gabby asked once we finally made it to her bedroom.

"I can take off my stuff, but I am not sure about my knee..."

"Don't worry about it. I'll do all the work."

Gabby undressed while I did my best to unrobe as well. I loved the way Gabby looked naked. It was so obvious she spent a lot of time in the gym. Everything was firm, tight, and in place.

Once I was on the bed, Gabby eased up beside me. I could tell she wanted to treat this like a random Bang or a jump-off, but I wouldn't allow it. I kissed her hard and passionately while running my fingers through her hair. I caressed, squeezed, and kissed her body in all the right places. Gabby was definitely not another one of my bones, so I was not going to treat her that way.

Next, she got on top of me like a cowgirl. Shit, I felt like I was the one being mounted. Gabby made sure the condom was properly on, and then she guided me inside.

"Sssss," she hissed.

Sex with Gabby felt so different. Much more soothing. Or maybe, I felt this way because I'd been banging Meghan for so long.

Gabby started to ride me passionately. She circled her hips slowly, just like I taught her. Sex with her was always amazing because everything she knew, she learned from me. So, she did sex just the way I like it. Just like my favorite fast food joint, Gabby knew what I liked, and she delivered. That was what I missed about her.

Don't get me wrong, sex with Meghan was awesome. It was just different with Gabby.

Softly, Gabby placed her hands on my chest as she rocked front to back, side to side, round and round, over and over again and again.

"Oh shit." I wanted her to know my satisfaction had arrived.

Gabby kept her eyes in contact with me the whole time. I was sure she saw my light going from flicker to dim to bright again. Yet, Gabby thrust her hips harder and harder. I could tell she wanted to remind me of what I'd been missing. But damn!

It didn't take us long to reach our climax. Once we did, we lay breathlessly side by side with long moments of silence. Gabby could stick a fork in Charlie Mo after that. I was done!

Then out of nowhere....

Pewwwwwww

"Oh my God!" she squealed.

I chuckled. Gabby passed gas as her body became relaxed.

"So embarrassing! I tried to hold it," she said while laughing at herself.

"It's all good."

"Thank God it didn't happen during sex," she said.

Gabby's slip-up was exactly what was needed to break the ice.

Afterward, we just lay there and talk for hours just like many times before.

Chapter
EIGHTEEN

"I hate it. I hate the job, and I hate the people!" Meghan complained.

"So, quit," I said.

"What? No! I couldn't quit. I was sure you want me out of here, so I do need my own money."

"Shut up. How many times do I have to say you can stay here as long as you need to?"

You really can.

After I got my trust fund, I would make sure Meghan was comfortable. Keeping things as "just friends" with both women has given me a new kind of freedom and a new outlook. But Meghan was winning the battle for my heart.

Honestly, it varied from day to day, but lately, Meghan made me feel as if we could have something forever. But damn, so did Gabby on most other days.

Regardless of the circumstances, Meghan remained sweet and loving while Gabby was more nonchalant. She was just not what she used to be. She showed affection, but she was not about to overdo it. But that was ok.

Gabby doesn't owe me anything.

Obviously, I was so confused!

"Meghan, like I said, you can quit."

"Oh, so you're gonna take care of me if I quit?"

"In case you haven't noticed, hell, I've basically been doing that for a while now."

Fool Me Thrice

"Oh, ok. I could help you with your business. Your birthday will be here soon. You'll get your money, then I can work for you," Meghan said.

My birthday was next month. My life was about to change, and I still didn't have my love life together. I was not afraid to admit having a woman around that loves me was probably the best way to go.

Yes, I was a mama's boy. I'll admit that. I was so used to depending on my mom. I was so used to receiving her guidance, knowledge, wisdom, words, and directions.

There's no doubt I needed a lady in my life. But I needed someone with a strong mind. I needed someone who was going to love me for me. Someone I could depend on.

There's no way I could go back to my old ways. I could no longer afford to continue with my routine of jumping from one money-hungry gold-digger to another. I was done with women that only want me for money.

Even though I had two amazing ladies in my corner, only one could go to the next level as my woman and my wife.

"I'll hang in there a little while longer and see how this job goes," Meghan said. She headed to the shower while I rushed out the door.

It was a Friday night and also Mrs. Vicki's birthday. They were having this big celebration at Tin-Can's house, and of course, I was invited. There was no way I was going to miss it.

Since I planned to down quite a few beers, Gabby was picking me up. With any luck, I would drink and drink until one of these ladies became a distant memory. That was my plan. That was how I would make my decision. Whoever faded away in my head would be the lady I left behind.

"You look good." Gabby complimented me as I opened her car door.

"Not as good as you," I returned and kissed her lips. She kissed me back.

The tight blue dress and dangling diamond earrings Gabby had on made me question my attire.

"Damn, you look really good. I feel like I am under-dressed."

"You're fine," said Gabby. "I'm pretty sure I was over-dressed, but I wanted it that way."

The weather was considerably warm. I wished I had worn my khaki shorts instead of long-legged jeans.

"Are you still thinking about starting a business," Gabby asked.

Now that was out of left field! I did tell her my plans to open a moving company awhile back. But she didn't know about the trust fund unless Tin-Can had shared it with her.

But I doubted it. Tin-Can would probably become my business partner eventually, so there were some things we would keep to ourselves.

I guess Gabby just assumes I'll try to do something special because of my frugal spending habits. Or maybe, she felt I have money left over from my botched inheritance. Yes, I do recall Gabby making previous comments about me pretending to be broke. But I never verified one way or the other.

"Sure. Within the next two months, I want to get something going."

"Charlie Mo, I've been thinking about opening a shop too. I love being a chef so much that lately, I've been thinking about doing more. I want to be more, you know?"

"Trust me. I do understand, dear."

Gabby and I talked about business all the way to her folks' house.

When we got to Tin-Can's house, the place was completely packed. There had to be at least fifty cars parked all over Tin-Can's yard.

"What do you want me to call you tonight," Gabby asked as I held her hand.

"Call me whatever you want. I'll roll with it."

We entered the house, and it was definitely set up for a huge party. Black and white balloons with streamers were all over the place. Black and white roses were on the tables. Nearly everyone was wearing black and white or pops of royal blue, including Gabby and me.

I'd seen black and white roses at many of dads' funerals, wakes, and memorials but never at a birthday celebration. It was quite odd to me. But oh well, it was Mrs. Vicki's birthday, and she could do as she pleased.

"Son," Tin-Can said as he hugged me. Then he embraced his daughter while beaming at the two of us. "Y'all look good together," he commented.

I gave Tin-Can my gift for the birthday girl. I spotted Mrs. Vicki across the room. She looked just so beautiful. I could see so much of her in Gabby.

"Man, most of these people are my wife's boring ass friends and her tired ass family," Tin-Can said as he led me away while Gabby went in the other direction.

"I couldn't even sneak downstairs like I want to. My wife will lose her shit," Tin-Can laughed.

"Uncle Stan," a voice came from behind him.

Both Tin-Can and I turned around.

"Charlie Mo?"

"Raven?"

Raven and I had a run-in when I was out splurging and going broke.

Raven was also a stripper. That was how I met her.

Raven was biracial. Even though her skin took after her white side, her body came straight from the "sista" side of the family. Raven's ass and tits are too much for the clothing she was wearing. She had no stomach, which was exposed by her crop top. If that wasn't tantalizing enough, she had juicy lips, firm legs, and a tiny waist that was similar to a remade of Jessica Rabbit.

Raven gave me a lap dance that made me take her home. I kept bringing her home time and time again until that trick stole $6,000 from me while I was sleeping.

"Y'all knew each other?" Tin-Can asked as he sips his drink.

"Barely. Did she say, 'Uncle Stan?'"

"Yeah. Her mama was married to my wife's brother. Why? Y'all messed around?"

"Briefly. But she didn't mean anything," I said in a very harsh tone. "Meantime, she still owes me $6,000."

Raven didn't comment; instead, she scrambled away.

"Gabby wasn't too fond of her anyway," said Tin-Can. "She wasn't blood, either," he added.

That was a close one, though. Tin-Can slapped my shoulder and continued greeting other family members.

For the rest of the night, if Tin-Can wasn't introducing me as his son, then Gabby was calling me her boyfriend. I was cool with it, though. I kept giving Gabby extra special attention because Raven couldn't seem to keep her eyes off me. Every time I touched Gabby, I could see the envy on Raven's face.

However, my initial plan of getting drunk and making a decision wasn't panning out. Tin-Can was hogging my time with meeting his relatives. So, I was not getting a chance to drink as much as I wanted to. Sadly, I still had two women in my head.

"Thanks for coming tonight," Gabby said as she drove me home.

"No problem. I had a good time."

"Me too," she responded.

We pulled up in front of my apartment building.

"I wish I could come in."

"You can, but you know Meghan still has the bedroom."

"Yeah," she said softly.

"I can go home with you if you want me to." I tried to assure Gabby my interest was with her and not Meghan.

"It's okay. I have to get up early in the morning anyway. I was serious about this business thing, so I need to start planning and doing my research. I will just call you tomorrow." I was so happy Gabby turned down my invitation to come inside.

So, I kissed Gabby long and gently before getting out of the car.

I headed towards the hallway but came to a stop. I made sure to duck out of sight as I watched Meghan come out of Ron's place and scurry back to mine.

"Look at this shit here," I said to myself.

Once the door closed, I continue straight to my apartment.

As soon as I was inside, I called Meghan's name.

She didn't answer, so I stepped into the bedroom. I found her in bed underneath the covers pretending to be asleep while faking a snore.

"Meghan?"

I wanted to see if she'd pretend to wake up. She didn't. She stuck to her charade.

What the hell was going on?

***

"Has Ron been calling you?" I ask the next morning.

"Yep. Every day," Meghan responds.

"Have you talked to him?"

"A few times," she responds honestly.

I guess I didn't have a right to feel jealous of Ron, but I did. After all, I did get my head beat in over Meghan's ass. It did bother me that Meghan would go back to this guy after what he put her through. Then, of course, she was putting up with me and all my mess with Gabby.

"But I didn't want him back. There's nothing there. He knows he lost a good woman. That is all," Meghan finished.

Fool Me Thrice

After that, she stopped talking.

I could definitely see why he wanted her back. Living with Meghan had given me a bigger appreciation unlike anything we had before. I saw a side far better than any relationship I had ever had.

"You got plans with your woman today?"

"Stop calling her that."

"What? Shit. You basically got two girlfriends."

"No, I don't," I confirmed.

"Whatever you say, Charlie Mo."

Meghan didn't say much else. She cleaned the dishes, got dressed, and was gone out of the door.

Probably going somewhere with Ron. I have to make up my mind. If I am not careful, Meghan will be out of my life once again. Hopefully, she is not at that point just yet.

Since Meghan wasn't around, I decided to give Gabby a call. I knew she talked about working on her business ideas, but I wanted to see if she would take a break for lunch with me.

Gabby agreed to meet me at one of her favorite spots, but that was a few hours away. I decided to make another attempt at the gym.

I stopped for a protein smoothie, and that was when I saw him.

Tin-Can.

I was about to approach him, but once he stood up, I saw a woman in front of him that wasn't Mrs. Vicki.

The two appeared to be arguing. Well, Tin-Can looked to be going the hell off about something. They were distant, so I couldn't hear anything. But moments later, Tin-Can stormed off, got into his truck, and sped away. The woman he was talking to immediately got on her phone then hurried to her car.

It was not my business, but Tin-Can didn't strike me as a cheater. His wife was amazing. Tin-Can seemed to love her more than anything in the world. Although, things are often not what they seem to be.

At the end of the day, it was Tin-Can's business. It was a little disappointing because I looked up to him. Plus, I wanted what he had. I wanted the house, the investments, the wife, and the kids. Tin-Can had become my new inspiration. There was always the possibility it was not what I thought, so I continued to the gym.

This time, I do a lot better than the last time with my workout. After forty-five minutes, I was back home.

When I passed by Ron's door, I could hear him shouting. So, I called Meghan immediately. She didn't answer. Next, I send her a text message. A few minutes later, she called me back and said she was on the way to the mall with a new friend from work. The only thing I could hear was music in the background.

There was no telling which woman Ron had in there. I shower, got dressed, then headed out to meet Gabby. She was already at the restaurant when I arrived.

She stood up to greet me. "Hey."

We both took our seats. "How is everything going with your research?"

"It's going. I think I want to get into real estate. I want to buy a few houses and flip them."

"You sound like your daddy."

"It's really a good market."

Fool Me Thrice

"Go for it."

"I really think I will," Gabby smiled.

"Let me know if you need me."

"What? Are you going to get out there and repair some of them?"

"If you need me to. Or, if you need a loan or something, I can help there as well. I got you."

I really meant those words. Whether we became an item or not, Gabby was someone I wanted to keep as a friend no matter what. So, I wanted her to know I would have her back if she needed me. Shit, I was not even sure why I said loan. If she needed something, then it was Gabby's to have.

"Okay," was all she said.

We ordered our food, and the next words out of her mouth surprised me.

"I'm still in love with you."

"Still?" I asked.

Gabby presses on, "I've been in love with you from the very beginning. I just didn't want to say it. Even before we had sex, I felt something for you. When all that stuff came up with Meghan, I felt really stupid for feeling the way I did so soon. But I do. I love you.

"Even though we have been in the friend zone because of that girl in your apartment, I still do love you." Gabby exhaled loudly. It was as though she could finally breathe.

I searched my heart for the right words.

"It's okay if you didn't feel the same. I didn't expect you to. I just wanted you to know how I feel."

I was delighted, but I felt like it was my turn to take the stage. The heat was on.

I touched Gabby's hand and said, "Gabby, I don't know if I've ever truly been in love before. I do feel like I loved you in another time and place. I have such a strong connection with you. I want you to be a part of my life, no matter what. that was for real."

Gabby smiled.

"You're an amazing woman. I've never met anyone like you. There are so many great things about you. I don't have time to list them all. I would be the luckiest man in the world if we ended up together. I knew I would."

I can tell Gabby appreciated what I was saying to her, so I kept going. I was not trying to spit game. I really wanted her to know that I think about her all the time. I felt she needed to hear it.

"Being around you makes me feel like I can do anything. Before I met you, I didn't feel like my life had a purpose. Now I do."

"So, I made you better?" asked Gabby.

"Honestly...yes. You really do."

That was the truth.

***

"What's wrong?"

Meghan's body was tense.

"Uh," she moved further away from me on the couch.

Fool Me Thrice

This was the first time she was acted this way towards me. We haven't had sex in about five weeks, but not by choice. Meghan was extremely tired most days because of her new work schedule. Plus, I've been spending a lot of time at Gabby's house and at the gym.

"I had sex with someone else the other day," Meghan blurted out!

I didn't expect that!

"Ron?"

"What? Hell no! A guy from work. I know we aren't together, but I just wanted you to know."

I didn't like the thought of another man touching Meghan. It made me angry, although I didn't have the right to be.

"Did you use protection?"

"Of course."

"You like him?"

"Nope," she said. "You had been sleeping over at Gabby's for a few days, and I guess I was jealous. He wanted me...so...."

I stepped in to soften some of Meghan's guilt.

"There's no reason for you to be jealous. Gabby and I are not having sex. I told you why I was there. After the gym, Gabby and I work heavily on our business ideas. We stay up doing research all night while bouncing ideas off each other."

Meghan listened to my plans, but it was different with Gabby. Gabby wanted to be successful just as bad as I did; whereas, Meghan didn't have the same drive.

I touched Meghan again. This time she didn't flinch.

"We seemed to be making progress for a moment, then suddenly it all changed. Charlie Mo, I am starting to think we aren't meant to be anything more than friends. Maybe, our story ended a long time ago."

"Please don't say that, Meghan." I pulled her closer.

I caressed the side of her face and waited for her to made eye contact with me. Once she did, I kissed her.

At first, Meghan didn't kiss me back. Then finally, the flood gates opened, and we were at it like horses out of the barn. We are kissing, hugging, and groping one another like it was a fire drill. Just when I started to rip off her clothes, Meghan stopped me.

"Charlie Mo, no more in between. If you want me, then it has to be just me. You have to end whatever you have going on with that Gabby woman. I mean it. Or...or I'm leaving," Meghan said.

I was somewhat shocked, but I knew it was just a matter of time before Meghan gave me an ultimatum. I could tell by the look on her face she was serious.

I was not sure if I could do what Meghan was asking. I knew I had a strong attachment to her and Gabby. But there's one thing Meghan was definitely right about – I had to choose.

"Okay," I said. Then I give Meghan a quick, simple but fuzzy answer. It was what she wanted to hear. "Sweetheart, it is just you and me now!" Yet, I was still unsure if would be Meghan in the end.

Chapter NINETEEN

"$40 on pump five."

I looked up at the sound of that voice. It happened to be the same voice I heard before I was ambushed over Meghan! I was sure of it. So, I turned around. It was the exact feature of the main thug who led that assault.

He walked out of the store. Instead of purchasing the things in my hand, I placed them on the counter and followed this roughneck out the door.

After being assaulted, I bought a pistol. I got my piece out of the glove compartment. It was about 10:00 p.m., and the store was deserted. So, I approached this punk with my gun held firmly in my hand.

"Let's see how tough you are without your boys," I said without getting too close to this hoodlum.

He turned around, and I pointed my pistol in his face.

At first, he acted as if he didn't know I was. He even looked confused.

"Y'all fools jumped me. But who's here to help you now? Huh?" I said with a deep gruff voice.

I was still pissed the hell off. Those bastards could've killed me!

"How much did Ron pay you? Huh? You willing to take this bullet for his ass?"

The guy held up his hands. "Ain't nobody named Ron paid me shit," he said. "Either you goin' to pull that damn trigger or get that gun out of my damn face."

I ignored him and kept my gun pointed in his direction.

"So, if Ron didn't send you and your homies to jump me, then who did?"

Fool Me Thrice

He shrugged his shoulders.

The clicking sound signaled his gas pump was finished. Slowly, he lowered his hands, took the nozzle out of his gas tank, and place it back where it belonged. Then he opened his car door.

"I asked you a goddamn question!" I kept yelling. Plus, I was still pointing my gun in his direction. Sirens in the distance told me the clerk had probably called the cops, and it was smart for me to leave.

Still, he didn't answer me. This idiot simply got into his car and sped off.

***

"I saw one of them," I said to Tin-Can at work the next day. "One of those fools that attacked me! I saw him!"

"Damn son! What did you do?"

"I pointed my pistol at him."

"Shit!" Tin-Can said.

"Yeah man. He still didn't say much. He just said he wasn't sent by the guy I thought set up the attack."

"You going to the police?"

"Nah," was all I said. The shit was over and done with. There was no telling who got problems with me. If it wasn't Ron behind the set-up, then it could have been anyone from my past. I would never know. "No police, though. I ain't no snitch."

Tin-Can chuckled.

"Well, I know you plan on opening up your own business pretty soon. So, I came across an investment that might be a good place for you to start. I plan to put about fifty G's in. It should return about half a million in profit."

"Oh really? You know my trust fund is right around the corner. Maybe I can try my hand at this investment stuff. I was trying to be like you, old man."

For the rest of our break, Tin-Can talked to me about different opportunities. He told me to think things over and let him knew which ones I was interested in. I had less than a month before my birthday and the release of my trust fund. I planned to stay a millionaire forever this time, especially with Tin-Can's help.

The days at work didn't seem as long and dreadful anymore. I guess it was because I wouldn't have to work so hard for too much longer. I clocked out each day with a smile on my face, and surprisingly, I was in a good ass mood most of the time.

At least until I got home.

"What's up, cuz," Ron said.

I kept walking.

"I know you ain't still salty because you think I had something to do with your ass beating. Like I said, if I wanted to mess you up, I would've done it myself."

"What the hell you want, Ron?"

He chuckled. "Damn cuz, it was like that?"

He followed me down the hall to my apartment.

"What my baby been doing?"

Fool Me Thrice

"You mean *my* girl?"

Ron squealed. "Oh, so she your girl now? What happened to all that friendship shit y'all were screaming? Huh?"

"Shit, you know what kind of woman Meghan is. Living with her made me see first-hand how special she is. I just couldn't pass that up to the next man. Not even to family." Especially an idiot like Ron.

I could see the anger all over his face.

"You think you doing something, don't you? You think you know Meghan because y'all were friends and all this bullshit. You don't know her. Not like I do. Trust me, she'll be back to me," Ron said as he backed away.

"I doubt it."

With that, I walked inside my apartment to find Meghan cooking dinner in just a t-shirt and a thong.

"Hey," she greeted me.

"Hey."

I called Meghan *my girl* to Ron just to get under his skin. But honestly, in a way, she was. At least as far as she knew. Meghan asked me to stop seeing Gabby. So, I lied to her and claimed I did.

But I didn't.

I had plans to meet up with Gabby at the gym a few minutes after I had gotten home. I was really trying to figure it all out, though.

Every single day I try to make up my mind. Just when I think I have the answer, the other girl does something amazing to make me lean her way.

"Was that Ron I heard?" Meghan asked.

"Yep. He still thinks he has a shot at getting you back."

"In his dreams," Meghan replied.

"You sure?" I asked.

"Well, not too long ago, I saw you coming out of Ron's apartment. Please tell me why?"

Meghan pretended as though she doesn't know what I was talking about.

"I was coming home when I saw you run out of Ron's apartment, and then you pretended to be asleep. I didn't bring it up because you can do whatever you want. But since..."

"I was stealing money," Meghan said.

"What?"

"Ron never took his key back. I saw him leave the complex that night. So, I went in and took some money out of his stash. I didn't want to kept asking you, and I really needed it. Ron had plenty of it tucked away. So, I knew he wouldn't miss it. Hell, he never ever counts it."

"All you had to do was ask me, Meghan."

"I know. At the time, things were weird between us. You were already doing enough. Besides...screw him! After all he put me through with those different women, hell, he owes me that. He better be glad I didn't take more than I did." The pork chops sizzled, and Meghan flipped them over.

It still didn't explain why she pretended to be asleep when I came in and called her name. But from the Meghan I used to know, I could tell she was truthful with what she told me.

"Well, you don't have to do that anymore. I got you," I said to her.

"I know," she responded.

Meghan finished cooking as I changed into my gym clothes. I told Meghan I would rather complete my workouts before I eat dinner. So, after a few more words, I headed out the front door.

Gabby was already at the gym and blowing my phone up. She wanted us to be so much more than what we were. Since I told Gabby I didn't have it in me to put Meghan on the streets, she offered me access to her place at any time. However, she was starting to notice that I had declined her offer every time she brought it up.

I didn't want to stay out all night with Meghan's ultimatum hanging over my head. At least, not until I was sure of who I was going to be with.

"Damn, you were supposed to be here like twenty minutes ago," Gabby complained.

"I know. I got caught up talking to my cousin."

"Uh-huh," Gabby said. "Have you sent Meghan back home to him? That is the only way I can start staying over. You know that, right?"

Gabby really wanted to be my girl. As a matter of fact, she brought it up all the time. The only difference was she hadn't given me an ultimatum like Meghan. I knew I was being pushed into a corner with the clock ticking.

If I wasn't careful, I would lose both of them and be back on my own once again. Because of these fears, I came up with a plan where I would admit nothing and deny everything then counter with accusations. This would be enough confusion to buy me the needed time to make a good decision.

"She was looking for her own place," I said rhetorically just to give Gabby some needed hope.

"Well, I said you could stay at my place while we try to work things out," Gabby said.

I didn't respond.

Quietly, we entered the gym. After walking on the treadmill for warm-ups, Gabby headed to the steam room while I moved over to the weights.

We met up thirty minutes later at the front door.

"Hello Gabrielle!" a woman said to her once we were outside.

Suddenly, I recognized the lady. It was the woman I saw Tin-Can arguing with not too long ago.

"Hi, Mrs. Housley. How are you?"

"I'm doing good, young lady," she said to Gabby. Then, she looked at me. "Hello. How are you, young man?"

"I'm good," I said in acknowledgment.

Mrs. Housley shook her head. "Well, tell your father to call me," she said to Gabby. Then she walked inside the gym.

"Who was that?"

"She is daddy's CPA. She keeps up with his money, investments, and stuff like that."

"I saw them arguing one day."

"They argue all the time," Gabby said. "She is the only one that can handle him, though. If things were just up to daddy, then he would have his money all over the place. She keeps him in line. She will tell him no in a heartbeat. But if you saw daddy and Mrs. Housley talking, then he's about to place his money into something lucrative."

I was glad she was just his business agent and not his mistress. I was so relieved because I really looked up to Tin-Can. He was the type of man I can only hope to be someday.

"You coming over?" Gabby asked.

"Yeah. I'll head home and get some clothes. Then I'll be there in about an hour."

"I'll cook and wait until you get there."

Now...what damn excuse can I give Meghan?

I took a shower as soon as I get home. When I came out of the bathroom, Meghan had a beer and warm food ready for me.

"That show you like comes on tonight," Meghan said while trying to find it on TV.

I tried to think of a good excuse to get out of the house. Since it was a weekday, I couldn't say I was going out to a bar. Suddenly, I received a text from Gabby asking if I was on my way.

Before I could figure out what to text back, Meghan sat down beside me. She placed my leg over her lap and started to rub my feet while I ate. Even with Meghan talking really fast about the TV show and giving me her thoughts, I could only think of Gabby.

Finally, I decided just to ignore Gabby's messages. I would tell her once I got out of the shower, I ended up dozing off on the couch. I would get up around two in the morning to text Gabby my apology.

"Charlie Mo? Are you listening to me?" Meghan smiled. I nodded back to her. With my mind all made up, I turn my phone face down, so I could give Meghan all of my undivided attention.

Chapter TWENTY

"Meghan, chill out, okay?"

"I just don't understand..."

"He was my friend first and my boss long before I even started talking to his daughter. Our friendship didn't end just because Gabby and I fell out."

It was Sunday, and of course, I was lying to Meghan.

I told her I was going fishing with Tin-Can instead of Sunday dinner at his house. If I didn't show up, Gabby would know something was up since I didn't show up like I promised her.

The other day Gabby barely believed I'd fallen asleep rather than coming over after my shower. I could tell she had her doubts, but she took it for what it was.

"I'll be home later. We are going fishing and then to the bar on the pier. You can call me at any time. I'll always answer, and you'll be able to hear Tin-Can." I knew there's a chance Meghan might call but bugging me wasn't her thing. I was just letting her know she can always reach out and touch me.

"I guess," was all Meghan said. Then she added, "My parents invited me over today."

"Your parents did what? You talked to them? Why didn't you tell me?"

Meghan shrugged. "I called my mom the other day. I told her I was done with Ron, and now I was living at your place. Of course, I got that lecture, but in the end, she asked me to come by. I wasn't sure if I was going to go, but I guess I will now."

Meghan's parents had a little money too. Not the kind my folks had, but they had money. I wouldn't call them rich, but they did make plenty. Both of her parents had good, high-paying jobs. As a matter of fact, that was how Meghan and I ended up at the same prep school.

But Meghan was as stubborn as a mule. Even back then, she just never liked being told what to do. She had always been that way. If I try to make her do something, then she'd do the exact opposite.

"I think it will be good for you to see your folks. Let me knew how it goes," I said. "Call me if you need me."

Afterward, I left the apartment and rushed towards Tin-Can's house.

"Hey," Gabby arrived only seconds after I did.

I gave her a big hug while we walked towards the front door but suddenly, she grabbed me by the arm.

"Charlie Mo..."

I smiled at her, but she had a look of confusion. Apparently, something was weighing heavily on her mind.

"What? What was it?"

She took a deep breath and started to speak, but she was interrupted by the sudden opening of the front door to Tin-Can's house.

"Hey y'all," her sister Violet chimed.

"Ay, what is it?" I asked Gabby.

She shook her head. "It can wait."

We walked inside, and the sweet aroma of Mrs. Vicki's food harassed my nostrils.

They greeted Gabby and me, then Tin-Can rushed me off to his man cave.

"You and Gabby seem to be working things out."

"More than anything, we're good friends," I said. "I think that was most important to the both of us."

"Yes. Friendships turn into the best relationships," he said.

His comment actually made me think less about Gabby and more about Meghan.

Tin-Can exhaled loudly. His breath smelled like sour baby milk and garlic. I couldn't wait for him to take a sip of his liquor to change the atmosphere.

"Oh, I got the numbers back for you." Tin-Can picked up his tablet from the bar. "Email this to yourself. When you come into your money, you'll be ready to roll."

"Alright. Bet," I said to Tin-Can.

I looked at the documents, but in my excitement to see Tin-Can and his family, I failed to forward the papers to myself.

"I'm proud of you, son. No pressure, but I am predicting you'll be my son-in-law someday soon."

Tin-Can laughed, then changed the subject. We talked and watched sports until called back upstairs.

"Congratulations are in order," Mrs. Vicki squealed out in excitement.

"Ma!" Gabby yelled.

"What?" I smiled at her.

Gabby mugged her mother.

"What was it?" Tin-Can asked.

"Well, since mama talks too much..." Gabby started. "My period was late!"

My heart dropped to the bottom of my stomach. Yes, there was a time where we had sex, and the condom did break. That shit had never happened to us before. We didn't realize it until the very end. At least I didn't, especially since Gabby was the one on top.

"I'm not saying I'm pregnant. I'm just late..."

A baby? Maybe? This changes everything. If Gabby is pregnant...Meghan and me...

There was no way in hell Meghan would stick around if Gabby turned out to be pregnant. She would haul ass with the quickness. I knew that for a fact.

Honestly, I couldn't blame Meghan either. I knew I would become closer to Gabby and the baby if such a thing did happen. Yes, I'd had this type of scare before, but Gabby was different. I could see myself married to her and having kids. I could see us forever.

"Well, when do we find out?" I just had to ask.

"If my period doesn't come, then I'll test at the end of this week," Gabby replied.

It was easy to see half of the room was filled with the joy of the possibility; whereas, the other half was full of awkwardness. I was in the awkward group.

"This is not the order I preferred, but I trust you will do the right thing by my daughter," Tin-Can finally said.

"Yes, sir," was all I can say.

Once we sat down around the table, the room filled with chatter.

Meghan called while on the way to her parents' home. I answered, just like I said I would. She asked if I was already at the bar. With all of the conversations taking place, I tried to be slick and say yes in a low tone.

Meghan told me she made it to her parent's house, and she would see me when I got home. As soon as I hang up the phone, I glanced at Gabby, who was looking directly at me.

"Who was that Charlie Mo? Your little girlfriend?" Gabby put me on blast in front of everyone, although I knew she still wanted an answer.

"Not my girlfriend but a friend. She just had a question. So, I answered."

"You talk to other women besides Gabby?" Mrs. Vicki asked. I guess it was her turn to throw me under that bus. Of course, Tin-Can already knew this arrangement, but now he was allowing it all to unfold before his entire family.

"She lives with him," Gabby answered. Instantly, everyone looked in my direction.

"Gabby! Really? Meghan and I have been close friends for years. She needed a place to stay, so I let her crash at my place. My mom called Meghan her second child. Meghan would do the same for me."

"Well, I told you. You can stay over at my place until she leaves, but you don't want to. You would rather be at home with Meghan," Gabby grunted.

"That's not true."

Maybe it is.

Gabby rolled her eyes while Tin-Can and Mrs. Vicki sipped their drinks.

"Anyway, I can't believe you might be having a baby," said Violet, changing the subject.

"You know you're wrong, right?" I complained to Gabby once we were outside. "You tried to be funny in front of your folks by mentioning Meghan."

"I wasn't being funny. It was what it is," Gabby said as we walk towards her car.

After Violet pulled me out of the fire, I was able to step away and return Meghan's call. That was when Meghan told me she would probably stay over at her parents' house. Yet, she promised to keep me informed of her decision.

"How do you really feel about my period being late," Gabby asked.

"Man, I don't know," I admitted. "I don't think I'm ready to be a father. But if you are pregnant, I'm not going anywhere."

"Oh. So, if I'm not, you're leaving me?"

"I didn't say that. I was just saying I got your back."

Gabby smiled. "Well, I would love to get it on with you tonight…like right now."

"Why are we still standing here," I asked while smiling at Gabby.

I helped Gabby into her car. "So, that was what you were trying to tell me before dinner?" I asked.

Gabby shook her head. "No."

"Okay, what were you trying to say?"

She stared at me.

"I'll tell you later," was all she said. So, I shut Gabby's door, and I got into my car to follow her.

Just as we arrived at Gabby's house, Meghan confirmed she'd stay at her parents' place for the night. Now, I knew I could spend time with Gabby without a rush.

Maybe tonight will be a game-changer one way or another. I need to make a decision and soon. But if Gabby was pregnant, then there's nothing more to say.

***

"I got to work this morning, and they told me to pack my things and leave!" Meghan called me about being fired from her job.

"What happened?"

Meghan puffed up and said, "That guy from work wanted to get with me again. I told him, no, but he kept trying anyway. Once he got the message, he started being nasty towards me. Then, he told my supervisor I kept making sexual advances towards him and making him uncomfortable. You see, he's important to the company. I was not."

"What kinda shit is that? Can they even fire you for something like that?"

"Apparently so, because they fired me," Meghan said as she continued to cry.

"Stop crying. Don't worry about it. You are gonna be alright. I got you. You can always find another job. If not, you're still gonna be straight. I'm going to make sure of that. I mean it."

Whether Meghan and I were together or not, I would make sure she was okay.

Meghan finally got off the phone, and I returned to my work truck.

"Everything okay?"

"Yeah.".

Tin-Can was overseeing me and two other men for the day. We stopped for lunch.

"Well, what are we doing for your birthday? We gotta go somewhere, Charlie Mo."

"Shit, you know I'm down! I am going to need that day off so I can process my trust fund.

"Bet. Are you sure you're not coming back to work?" Tin-Can asked.

"Nah. But I'm going to be smart when I get the money in my hand." I laughed. "Oh, I plan on giving you 100k to invest. What do you think?"

"Shit, $100,000? You ain't playing around, Charlie Mo. I was thinking you might do about $10,000 to start."

"Shit, Stan, you'll have more to play around with," I said.

"I'm down to show you how to make more money. I'll be ready."

I was surprised Tin-Can even needed a CPA. He was so good with numbers. He showed me knacks for budgeting and how his money had tripled in a matter of months from different investments. I would've never guessed Tin-Can needed someone to help him work a deal. Still, I couldn't wait to get mine.

It had been a while since I contacted all the representatives for the release of my trust fund. The funds had been sitting in a lockbox, waiting for me to reach that designated age.

"Shit, I was thinking Vegas," said Tin-Can.

"Yeah, let's do it!" I said.

After we finished our workday, I stopped to get flowers and strawberries to take home to Meghan.

"Hey, pretty lady," I said to her.

She smiled.

I was going to miss coming home to Meghan if Gabby was pregnant. I felt somewhat sad. I knew I would have to let Meghan go if I was having a baby with Gabby. I knew I was being selfish, but I didn't want to lose either one. For the first time, I had finally found two women who were not gold-diggers.

"Thank you!" She reached for the flowers and the chocolate-covered strawberries. "I really don't want to be a burden," Meghan said.

"What? Chill out. You're not. You'll find something else. Or, you can help me with my business like you said. Shit, you can work for me. I wouldn't fire you." Then I laughed.

Meghan laughed too.

"On top of that, I don't feel good today. I feel nauseous."

"You ain't pregnant, are you?" I asked while giving a guarded smile.

Meghan and I have always used protection. As far as I knew, I had never had a condom to break with Meghan. Yet, I was scared as hell. This could be the scariest shit I had faced since God knows when.

"No, fool! It might be something I ate. Or maybe, I am about to get sick. I don't know," Meghan explained.

Whew! Thank you, Lord!

Meghan sat the flowers on the table and put the strawberries in the refrigerator. Then she snuggled up to me on the couch.

"I love you, Charlie Mo."

Meghan always went out of her way to make sure I knew how she felt about me. There was something about the way she said it.

I knew for sure Meghan loved me.

"Well…I love you too," I said to her.

I really think I do.

***

"Negative," Gabby said after showing me the pregnancy results. I couldn't tell if she was happy and relieved or sad and disappointed.

"Well, that was a good thing. Right?"

Gabby shrugged. "I guess so since you don't know if you want to be with me."

"Here we go again," I rolled my eyes with a smile.

Internally, I was relieved she wasn't pregnant. Yet, I was still confused about which woman I was going to pick. However, I was glad I could make my decision based on my heart and not out of obligation

"I did something for you today," Gabby said.

She presented me with a package wrapped in brown paper.

"I don't know if you will like it, but I wanted to do something special for you. I believe in you, Charlie Mo. I want all of your dreams to come true."

"What's this?"

"Open it and see."

I ripped off the paper. It took a moment for me to figure out what I was staring at. It was a framed picture. But not just any old picture. It was a picture of a picture. It was an image that contained a photo of my parents and me. However, this picture was much more enhanced. It was more artistic looking. All of the features had been redrawn and embellished. Underneath the artwork reads, "Fullers Moving Company: The Truck and Fuel Behind Your Next Move."

"I know you couldn't decide on a name for your new business, so I decided to help. I had this logo created for you. What do you think? Do you like it?"

I looked at this new creation and smiled back at Gabby. Then I glanced at the oversized logo once again. I had been keeping that photo in my car. At some point, Gabby must have taken a picture of it.

My parents would have loved this. This would have made them so proud.

"I love this. Man, I really do. You didn't have to do this for me. It was so perfect. Just like you."

Gabby smiled.

"I've never had anyone do something like this. I've never had anyone like you." I placed the picture on the marble countertop and walked closer to Gabby.

"You changed me. You made my life better. You brought me back to life!" I may have been going back and forth with my thoughts, but my heart was leading the way. "Gabby, I need you in my life. I need you for the rest of my life. This journey won't be worth it without you."

Fool Me Thrice

I knew I sounded like a love ballad, but I didn't care. Gabby had touched my heart and repaired my soul. This lady had a heart of gold, just like my mama. No doubt, I found a real jewel this time.

"You sound like you love me, Charlie Mo?"

"I do. I love you, Gabrielle." I called her by her real name.

"I love you too, Prince Charles Fuller."

In a span of two days, I have told Gabby and Meghan I truly loved them.

But I really do. I love them both.

But I couldn't have two wives. I didn't know what in the hell I was going to do.

Dean Conan

Chapter TWENTY-ONE

"**M**eghan, what do you want to do?

"You mean my dream job?"

"Yes," I nodded.

"I want to help kids. I am willing to work at a youth center or a daycare. I just know I want to work with children."

"What if you could start your own business? What would that be?"

"Hmmm...I don't know. Why?"

"Because Meghan, if I can help, then I want to make some of your dreams come true."

My birthday was a week away, which meant my entire life was about to change...again. Meantime, I was still comparing Gabby and Meghan in every way possible. Some days I felt Gabby was the perfect one for me. Then other times, I felt Meghan would be better in the long term. I couldn't explain it.

Gabby was literally everything I can ask for. She really keeps to her plans. At the same time, Meghan was so undecisive but totally lovable to the core.

In a weird way, Meghan reminded me of Evelynn. She wasn't similar at all to Meghan, but she was someone I came close to marrying.

I dated Evelynn right after my folks' tragedy. Meghan didn't like her, and she didn't like Meghan. Yes, Meghan had that feeling in her bones about Evelynn being nothing more than a Gold-digger. Foolishly, I never accepted Meghan's advice.

Evelynn was never quiet or subdued. She was always straight to the point. I was younger and assumed Evelynn had more focus on life than I did. Yet, nothing was ever good enough. I bought Evelynn purses that had to be returned because they weren't Louis Vuitton. Her shoes had to be Alexander Wang or Mau Miu. Her coats had to be mink.

If that wasn't enough, Evelynn wanted things just to made Meghan jealous. No matter where we went, Evelynn would purposely overwork the help just to show her importance. Then she would make me pay in cash so everyone could see my Benjamins. Still, I put up with Evelynn and her nasty ways because of her sexual appetite. She was just a home-grown freak with no off button.

Sadly, I was a goldfish to her salacious body. I just couldn't get enough while Evelynn kept me glued to her ass like a cheap stamp. I knew it was crazy, but I thought Evelynn was the wife for me. I really thought she loved me.

But after I lost the last of my inheritance, Evelynn said she needed to leave before I break her heart. It was so obvious my empty pockets had taken her love away. Before I knew it, Evelynn had skipped out of town, and I never saw her again.

I learned the hard way that gold-diggers didn't fool around with potential. They messed with money. But on-the-other-hand, Meghan had genuinely stood by me. If anything, I was the idiot that ignored Meghan during my days of sunshine.

I knew if I made that mistake again, Meghan would not be around for the third time.

"I don't need any of your trust fund money, Charlie Mo. I can just be your cute ass wife helping you run shit," Meghan laughed. "You can just keep me looking good and feeling good, and that will be enough for me."

That may have been somewhat funny, but I was certain Meghan meant it.

"What do you want to do for your birthday?"

"The day of...well, I don't know. I'll be checking on my trust fund for sure. But that was also the weekend Tin-Can and I are going to Vegas."

Meghan nodded. "Well, I got a little something planned for you that night. I'm just making sure you know." Then Meghan winked at me and walked away just as my phone started to ring.

"Hey, baby."

"What's up, Gabby?"

I was still amazed at the emblem Gabby designed for my company. That creation made me adore her little ass even more.

"I'm outside. Is this a good time to come in?"

Suddenly, I got a lump in my throat and instantly jumped to my feet.

"Hell no. She is sick as hell. I'm headed out anyway."

I lied to Gabby and told her I was on my way to my car. Meghan wasn't sick anymore, but she would lose her shit if Gabby came inside. That was just asking for trouble. Plus, I had Meghan convinced we were no longer dating.

Not to mention, I finally got Gabby to think Meghan and I were just friends. With that, Gabby decided to accept Meghan as a friend, too. But, I knew not to ever say the word "relationship" when speaking of Meghan.

"Baby, I'll be back in a few!" I yelled out to Meghan.

"Okay!" Meghan yelled back from the bathroom.

I made it outside, and Gabby was parked right beside my car.

Fool Me Thrice

"She got the whole house smelling like ammonia. She is as sick as a dog."

Gabby got out of her car and immediately started to hug me. I kissed her.

Nervously, I looked around, knowing Meghan was right inside the apartment. This was just too close to home.

"Where you going?" Gabby asked.

I glanced down at my phone as if I had somewhere to be.

"I gotta made it to the bank before it's too late. You knew they close at 1 on Saturdays."

Gabby nodded.

"We can go to lunch afterward. Come on, dear."

Gabby got back into her car and followed me to the bank. Initially, I didn't need cash but getting away from my apartment building was a must.

I went to the inside ATM to take out $300.00 knowing I'd be loaded in a week.

"What you want for lunch?"

"Something good."

Neither of us had an appetite, so we strangely stopped at Gabby's parents' home. I ended up working with Tin-Can around the yard while Gabby helped Mrs. Vicki in the house.

"Spring cleaning in the summertime," I said to Tin-Can. He was getting the yard altogether as if he was remodeling the place. He had all kinds of stuff on the side of the road and landscapers remaking the grounds.

"Out with the old, in with the new," he said. "You will have a big ass house once again, Charlie Mo."

I shrugged. "I'm not sure if I'll start out like that. I was thinking of a condo first. Then whenever I am ready to settle down, I can rent it out and pocket the income."

"I've taught you well," Tin-Can beamed. "Smart thinking, son. Smart thinking."

Around six o'clock, I told Gabby I had to get back to see if Meghan needed additional medication. Gabby was ok with my concerns since Meghan was supposedly sick.

Once I walk into the apartment, I saw Meghan's bags by the door. *This is strange.*

"Meghan!" I screamed.

"Meghan!"

She came into the living room.

"What are you doing?"

"Ron showed me the video of you kissing Gabby today. You were right outside the apartment too!" Meghan shook her head in disbelief. "You lied to me, Charlie Mo. You told me whatever you and Gabby had was over. But you lied!" Meghan screamed. "I should've known you wouldn't leave that skank alone. I should've known." Then she disappeared into the next room.

"Meghan. It ain't like that."

"It ain't like what, Charlie Mo? Kissing her ain't like what? Please explain."

Shit, I can't.

"You're in love with two women. I am not sharing no man no more. I've had enough of that shit!"

"Meghan, where are you going to go?"

"Home to my parents. I'll figure out what's next from there. Now that Ron is out of my life, I can live at home again.

I could tell Meghan had been crying. Breaking Meghan's heart was never my intention.

"Meghan, please don't leave. I don't want you to go."

She came back and stares at me.

"Ok, then. Call her! Right here. Right now. Call her and tell her you can't see her anymore. Call her and tell her whatever the two of you have was over."

I fondled back and forth with my phone.

"There's a way to do things. This isn't the way. I will tell Gabby. But honey, not like this. I didn't want to hurt either of you. Yes, I've been lying to both of you. But please let me do it my way."

Meghan shook her head. Then out of nowhere, she screamed, "Man, The HELL WITH YOU!"

Meghan stormed off with me on her heels.

"The way you love me, I can't explain it, but I need it. I need you, Meghan."

"No, you don't need me. You got her. Just like before. Once you get one of those gold-diggers, you don't need me anymore." I heard Meghan's voice starting to crack, and soon after, she began to cry.

"You'll have your money. You can have your chick just like last time. I'll move on just like the other times."

"Meghan, baby…"

"No! Don't touch me. If I knew you were going to do this, I would have stayed with Ron!"

Meghan swatted at my hand and grabbed her purse.

"I'll just come back and get the rest of my shit while you're at work." Meghan looked back just as she reaches the front door.

"Meghan. Please…"

"Goodbye, Charlie Mo," she sobbed. "For real this time!"

"No! Please! Don't go!"

***

"Where's my baby?" Ron sarcastically asked, then laughed loudly.

"Oh, I already know. I saw her moving her shit out while you were at work." He sounded so amused. "I knew it wasn't going to work. I knew that shit. You got caught up, Charlie Mo. By the way, you look good on video. Did you think I was gonna just sit back and let you have her? Huh? Did you? You ain't no better than me. You think you are, but you're not. You've never been no more than Charles THE Moron. We both lose this time, Prince Boy."

Just as I was about to punch Ron in his big, fat mouth, he slammed his door in my face. But Ron was right. All of Meghan's stuff was gone. Meghan was gone. She wouldn't answer any of my calls, either.

Almost immediately, I noticed how different the place was without Meghan. The vibe was different. The smell of the house was different.

Man, I really messed the hell up.

Fool Me Thrice

"Hey babe, what are you doing?" Gabby chimed.

"Nothing. What's up?" I was pretending not to be sad.

"Open the door. I'm not taking no for an answer this time. I made dinner for all three of us. If Meghan was that important, well, I'll try to be her friend too. You see, I am not going anywhere no time soon."

When I opened the front door, Gabby walked in carrying bags of food.

"Meghan doesn't live here anymore. She moved out." I was trying my best not to sound disappointed.

"What happened?" Gabby asked.

"It was just time for her to go."

Gabby started to place the food on the counter.

"Well, in that case, it is dinner for two," Gabby shrugged.

"Maybe, her moving out was for the best. This can be a new start for us, Charlie Mo. Plus, it makes it easier to trust you."

Then Gabby turned on music while preparing our meals.

Gabby was in such a good mood that it made it hard for me to mope around. But as the night went on, heavy thoughts of Meghan kept flooding my head. It didn't matter how much Gabby talked and made me laugh, I couldn't stop thinking of Meghan.

It's weird, but it appeared I really screwed things up this time.

Dean Conan

Chapter TWENTY-TWO

Dean Conan

"I love you, Charlie Mo. I'll see you later."

I could tell Gabby was smiling on the inside.

After hanging up the phone, I found myself sitting in my car, staring at the building of HCS.

This was my last day of work. As long as everything went as planned, I'd be outta there.

My birthday was tomorrow. It was a new day, but I would be rich again. The thought of it made me uneasy. Almost scared. I was afraid of the man I might become again.

I'm not sure why I went to work that day. I didn't need to be there, and I didn't want to either.

"Yes, son," Tin-Can said on the other end of the phone. "You need this one off, too, huh?" He laughed knowing my plans to quit once I got my money.

"Yeah man. I'm outside, but I don't want to come in. My head just isn't right this morning.

"Alright. Take the day. I am sure there are some things you want to go through before your life changes tomorrow. Call me if you need me," Tin-Can said.

I'd gotten my car repaired. But after the attack, it hasn't been the same. Honestly, once I got my money, I was going to see if Tin-Can still wanted to buy it. I didn't need all the attention anymore. I just wanted a better life, a legacy. I wanted to do something that would make my parents proud.

As a reminder, I drove over to my old neighborhood. I had an urge to see my old home once more. My daddy built this massive place right across the street from the funeral home. It all belonged to someone else

Fool Me Thrice

now. A more affluent buyer purchased the house, the building, and the hearses right from under me. It was called Lester's Mortuary and Family Park.

After driving for over thirty minutes, there it was. The house. The parlor. They looked better than ever.

Seeing it brought back so many memories. Not many of my dad, but a ton of great moments with my mom. But there was one where my mom and dad joined me on a rug by the fireplace. I couldn't have been any older than eleven or twelve.

I was watching a movie with a big bowl of popcorn, and then out of nowhere, my parents came to sit with me. They snuggled close and said they loved me. They went on to say how proud they were, and I was the best thing that ever happened to them. Then we watched movie after movie. We ate far too many bowls of popcorn before falling asleep on the floor.

I remember waking up in the middle of the night, only to see my parents on each side of me. They were still holding hands just above my head. I'd never felt so safe and so loved. That was one of my favorite times with them. Yet, it was a rare event where daddy showed his love for me.

Another unlikely occasion of my father's love was when I nearly lost my virginity. I was forced to share that experience with my dad. I definitely didn't want to tell mom. She would have flipped out because she was always so worried about girls chasing after me because of my connection to their reputations. So, I confided in my dad.

He took a day off from work when he noticed me sneaking into the house with my stained summer wear from zipper to pocket and pocket to zipper. He knew I was friends with Becky, but that was all. He never asked if we were intimate, and I never said anything to make him or my mother think otherwise. They were kind of confused about how Becky and I were friends even though Meghan had always been around. I was so embarrassed when daddy caught me with soiled white shorts.

He smiled at me. He kinda knew what it was, but he asked anyway. So, I fessed up and told him. I said, "Dad, after Becky and me left The Burger Bend, we went back to her place. We would normally kiss and grind, but this time Becky was more aggressive than normal. She actually took my tool out of my pants and put it in her mouth. I was at such a loss because we had more than enough snacks to settle our appetites.

"Still, I didn't say anything until I got this sensation I was about to pee. I didn't want to embarrass myself in front of Becky, so I pushed her head back, grabbed my clothes, and sprinted toward home just to save face. But dad, as you can see, I didn't make it. I flooded my underwear and my shorts on my way here. So, please didn't tell mamma. I would clean all of this myself!"

Daddy couldn't stop laughing at me. That was when he explained sex and blow jobs to me. I was so impressed and overwhelmed by how he understood my ignorance to intimacy.

"Good sex can be dangerous, son. A woman with good skills can either made or break a man. Make sure you find a woman who has more than just good sex. You want a woman who makes you feel good in and out of the bedroom. You have so much inside of you. There's so much in store for you. I need you to be smart, son."

"You know how much I love you. I would give anything to make sure you're okay. I would die so you could live. So always be smart. Always be aware. Be careful of the doors you walk through and the women you

Fool Me Thrice

lay with. There are some real snakes and some real gold-diggers out there. Always be alert.

"Yes, there are some scandalous women in this world, and don't you ever forget that."

After that, he took me outside to play basketball while he gave me better details of handling myself the next time. He told me to always wear protection. Then he told me not to tell mom about the advice he had given me.

I'll never forget that day. He kicked my ass in one-on-one, but I didn't mind. I was just happy to be spending time with him. I knew driving down memory lane would bring a few tears, but I really did need it.

Man, I miss my folks.

∗∗∗

"Happy birthday!"

Gabby woke me up as she brought the tray closer to my bed.

"I think I overdid it," she complained.

Damn. She did. She had pancakes, sausage, bacon, eggs, grits, liver pudding, and toast.

"Damn baby. Thank you," I said as I kissed her.

Then she climbed in bed beside me.

"Are you going to work today?" Gabby asked.

"No. I have some running around to do."

I still hadn't told Gabby about the trust fund party. I was planning to surprise her with a check for her new business venture. She had never asked me for anything. Not one dime or one red penny. Yet, she didn't mind going out of her way to do things for me. It was my turn now.

We'd spent a lot of time working out the details of our start-up companies. We were always playing with numbers. It appeared Gabby needs around $75,000 to get her business off the ground.

I was going to give her $100,000 just in case. That was more than enough. Nothing could measure to what Gabby had done for me, mentally, so that would be a good statement.

"What do you want for your birthday," Gabby asked. "I've been trying to decide what to get you, but I'm not sure. I give up. So, I'm asking you, Charlie Mo."

I wonder if Meghan is going to call me today.

She wasn't taking my phone calls. She wasn't responding to my text messages, either. She was just… gone. There was nothing I could do about it except to move on.

"You." I finally replied.

"What?"

"All I want for my birthday and for every birthday after this one…is you." Gabby beamed.

"If it wasn't official before, I want to make it clear now. Gabby, I love you. I want you to be mine. My woman, my wife, and hopefully, the mother of my kids one day soon."

The big day was here. I was so glad to have a woman that loves me by my side. I was not going to pretend as if I didn't.

Secretly, I wasn't sure I would have chosen Gabby if Meghan was around. But Gabby was still one hell of a catch. It was a blessed choice that I would be absolutely happy to live with.

Gabby threw herself up against me. She almost knocked over the breakfast tray. She hugged my neck tightly and squeezed.

"I didn't expect to fall in love with you," she whispered. "Loving you wasn't a part of the plan."

"Oh, so you had a plan?" I chuckled.

"Yes," Gabby said while holding onto my neck!

Finally, she let go. Then we had sex for about an hour. Afterward, Gabby headed out to handle her business, and I did the same.

Dean Conan

Chapter TWENTY-THREE

"**H**appy birthday, son." Tin-Can called to greet me, but Gabby beat him to it. Of course, I'd given up on Meghan wishing me anything except to say, "Charlie Mo, kiss all of my ass." But so far, that hadn't happened.

The trust fund was officially mine. It would take a few days for everything to be processed, but all the paperwork was complete. I was officially a millionaire again.

"The Mrs. made you a cake. Can you pick it up at my place after work?" Tin-Can asked.

"Sure. Oh, if you still want to buy this car..."

"Shit, shoot me the price, and I'll take it off your hands. I'll give it to Violet," said Tin-Can.

We talked for a few minutes more as I drove up to my apartment building. When I approached the complex, there were cops everywhere. Ron was being led to a police car. I could see dogs sniffing everything, so I was sure it was drug-related.

I hadn't spoken to Ron since he filmed me kissing Gabby. Yes, it was still my fault, but he was too damn happy to come between Meghan and me.

After proving I lived in the building, I was allowed to go inside my apartment.

"Hey."

She startled me as I walked in the door.

Meghan.

My heart skipped a beat.

Man, was I happy to see her face! I just wanted to tell her how sorry I was.

Fool Me Thrice

"Happy birthday."

"Thank you. How have you been? Why are you here?"

I was just so excited to see Meghan. She wasn't telling me "what I need to kiss." However, if she displayed that little brown ass out of contempt or lustfulness, then I would most definitely fulfill her request.

"Are the police still out there?" she asked.

"Yeah. They're taking Ron's ass to jail."

"I know," said Meghan. "I turned that fool in. I called and told them he had drugs and illegal guns in his apartment. I even stated I heard a woman screaming," Meghan added as she glanced down at the floor.

Next, Meghan went deeper and said, "Ron showed up yesterday acting a damn clown. He told me I would never be happy if I wasn't with him. My daddy went outside and tried to get him to leave, but Ron punched Daddy in the face and broke his nose. I'm just sick of his thuggish shit! So, I called the police on his ass."

I could tell Meghan didn't feel bad about what she had done. Shit, neither did I. I was impressed at how diabolical she had been. I had never seen that side of her.

Then Meghan said, "I remembered I still had your house key. I just came by to say happy birthday and..."

"And what...?" I cut in. "Please go on. Do you miss me? If you do, say it. Because I damn sure miss you, Meghan."

But instead, she said, "I need to inform you about that skank you picked over me."

"What? Why now?" I asked.

"Remember you told me about pulling a gun on this guy who attacked you?"

"Yeah."

"You told me he drove an orange old skool car that had a black stripe along the side with a custom-made tag featuring a basketball."

I certainly did tell that to Meghan. I studied that car as he drove away from me at the store. I could've easily given those details to the police. I was sure they could've found out exactly who he was. But like I said, I ain't no goddamn snitch.

"What about this thug, Meghan?"

She hesitated but not for long.

"I saw Gabby talking to that same dude today. They were leaning up against his car and talking as though they are friends or something. If I had to guess, Gabby had something to do with the way that attack went down.

"It looked like they beat your ass for playing Gabby and keeping me around. It appears Ron didn't have anything to do with it just like he said." Meghan pulled out my house key and continued, "Like I said, you picked the wrong girl. She was just using you. That bitch! I really hope her coochie grows together."

"Say what?" I was floored by her statement. "Meghan, what the hell?"

For all the shit she had done, her vajayjay needed to be stitched up." This time I laughed for sure. But Meghan never cracked a smile.

The next thing out of her mouth was, "Happy birthday Charlie Mo." She sounded so disappointed.

Meghan dropped my key in my hand and stood on her tiptoes to kiss my cheek.

"Meghan! Wait! Stay! What if I choose you? Can I still choose you?"

She didn't answer me. Meghan walked out the door without looking back.

As soon as she was gone, I called Gabby. I told Gabby I ran into one of the guys who jumped me at the store. But I didn't give her all of the.

Gabby and I had rebuilt our relationship faster than expected. Since Meghan hadn't been around to come between us, we had opened up new channels to our bond. But after telling Gabby this startling information, she didn't seem bothered. For damn sure, she didn't admit to knowing the people involved.

Gabby deflected and said, "I was just about to call you. Daddy told me you are coming to the house. I'll meet you there."

I forgot about the cake. I wanted to ask Gabby more about this hoodlum, but she rushed off the phone.

A few minutes later, I headed over to Tin-Can's house. I was so messed up. If Gabby got old boy and his crew to jump me, then I probably shouldn't be dealing with her. Yeah, I probably got what I deserved for playing two damn good women, but that was still some lowdown shit.

"I'm gonna give you this check, but man, don't cash it just yet," I said to Tin-Can.

Even before I got my hands on my money, I was working to make sure I got off on the right track. I gave Tin-Can a check for $100,000.

No matter what I found out about Gabby, I wanted to make sure I didn't end up broke again.

"I'll make sure I get this where it needs to be. You can be sure I'll get you some paperwork before investing this money." Then Tin-Can put the check into his back pocket.

"Come on," he said while leading me to the kitchen.

Shouts of Happy Birthday came from everyone, including Gabby. I returned a heartfelt "thanks" to all involved. On the table was a spread of my favorite delights, plus Mrs. Vicki's chocolate cake.

"Y'all didn't have to do this."

"You're basically a part of this family now," Tin-Can said, as he tapped me on the back. "You don't have any relatives to help celebrate your day, but you got us."

"I really do like being a part of this unit. I love the feeling. I really do."

Gabby walked closer and kissed me. I kissed her back.

"Can we talk outside for a minute," I said to Gabby.

Mrs. Vicki prepared my plate while Gabby and I stepped out the back door.

"I'm gonna ask you something just once. I don't need you to bullshit me. Just kept it real," I said to Gabby.

Suddenly, Gabby's face shows an air of concern.

"Did you set that shit up for me to get jumped? I saw you talking to that fucker who I know had something to do with it!" Of course, I was lying, but I didn't want to put Meghan in this.

"Charlie Mo... Baby."

"Did you plan that shit?" I interrupted Gabby.

"Yes," she admitted in a soft voice. "But I didn't set it up. That is the wrong word. He chose to do it, and I couldn't talk him down." Gabby started to spill her guts.

My chest grew tighter and tighter as I tried to breathe. I couldn't tell if I was angry, hurt, or a mixture of both.

Fool Me Thrice

"He's a friend. He's an old friend. Daddy would never approve of me being with someone like him, so we were always just friends. I was angry. I was so hurt that I told him what you did to me. I told him you made me fall in love with you while all along you were screwing some other skank.

"He told me he was going to step to you like a real man. I asked him not to do such a thing. But he told me nothing I could say would stop him from confronting you. I really thought he was just going to drop it after I finish sharing my frustrations. I swear! I had no idea he was going to do all of that to you. I didn't even know he planned on jumping you. I thought, at best, he was going to say a few words and be on his way.

"You gotta' believe me. I didn't know he was going to get his boys to help him attack you. I would've never said anything to him if I even thought he would do something crazy like that," Gabby pleaded.

"Wow..."

I took a step back from her.

Gabby had more. "After daddy told me you were in the hospital, I called and asked why he did that. He told me he whipped your ass, and you better not hurt me again. He was so pissed about how you treated me, and I was so mad at him for assaulting you."

"Obviously not! You were with him today!"

"Today is the first time I've seen him since I found out what he did. We just happened to be at the same place at the same time. It was my chance to call him on his bullshit face to face. He did admit to going too far. Basically, he said it was all because of his feeling for me."

Gabby never took her eyes off me. She kept eye contact the whole time, which made me feel like she was being truthful.

"I'm sorry. I didn't know it was going to go down like that. I swear. I wanted to talk to you about this ordeal, but I didn't know how. I didn't want you to blame me. I didn't want you to think I wanted him to do anything to you because I didn't.

"I was mad at you at the time, but I didn't want you to get hurt. I was so ashamed my words may have caused it. I wasn't going to bother you again after seeing you at the hospital. But Daddy really, really, likes you. He encouraged me not to give up on us if I truly felt we had something special."

"Wait, Tin-Can knew!?! What the hell??!?"

"No, daddy didn't know," Gabby said. "But I did tell him I was just going to leave you alone. He would lose his shit if he knew I was the cause of you being put in the hospital. Man, in his mind, you're practically his son-in-law. I am so sorry. I didn't mean for all that to happen to you. I really didn't."

After Gabby came clean, I didn't know what to feel. I was just standing and searching myself for my own answers. I hadn't felt this betrayed since my last gold-digger named Tang Newton.

Tang was every man's delight. This woman had a body that made everything she wore look lascivious. Church attire, business wear, Halloween costumes, and especially swimwear. She just always appeared to have a lecherous look about her. I knew that kind of body could get every damn dollar I had. After meeting me, she decided to stalk me day after day. She just always knew where to find me.

The girl really did her homework. I was sure she saw money flowing out of my ears. So, she smartly turned the dial up a few extra notches. Since sex was my calling card, Tang had to have known I would answer that bell. Finally, she went hard in the paint and told me, "Men like to have sex with me for good luck."

Fool Me Thrice

After that, I was powerless and quickly jumped on board. My success was fading, so why not spin that wheel with Tang. It wasn't long before I found out Tang was as freaky as advertised.

Tang promised not to bite if I dated her, yet she loved for me to dig my teeth into her alien body. She would even make me take her panties off with my mouth. She tried to warn me about how addictive she was. I thought she was being cute and conceited.

Tang said, "After I get you home, you will call me Tang-A-Lang." Well, she screwed me like it was a challenge. It was a contest where I took many losses. As a matter of fact, I always lost.

Tang would make me spell her name while she was breaking me off. But I was never able to assemble all the letters in the correct order. There was just no way to complete her assignment with all she had going on. I was easily the biggest screamer in that relationship. I actually started calling her Tang A Lang just like she predicted.

But Tang failed to warn me about her other love affairs and offbeat situations. I came to find out she had married men, female admirers, and absolute fools like me. Tang-A-Lang was also using my money to assist her less fortunate lovers. I even tolerated that for a minute. We were all fighting for her time. Literally. I was tackled not once but twice by a football player, sucker-punched by a dwarf-sized boxer, forced to floss and gargle a 9-millimeter by an angry drug dealer, bum-rushed by some rappers, and finally sliced open by a jealous female lover.

No doubt, Tang-A-Lang had that animalistic attraction that brought us all in like hyenas to a carcass. It was all too much for Charlie Mo. I swore I would never date another woman that caused me to put my ass on the line like Tang-A-Lang.

Before this shit, Gabby couldn't do any wrong in my eyes. If she was being honest, I guess she still hasn't really crossed me. If she didn't know her thug friend was going to jump me, could I really fault her for it?

"I love you, and I didn't want you to be mad at me. I should've told you once I found out my friend, Dickie Beale, and his gang did that shit. Hurting you was never something I wanted."

Gabby started to cry.

"Holy shit! Did you say Dickie Beale was in on this too?"

That's the motherfucking classmate that ran my folks down. It wasn't enough for him to kill my parents. He wanted to mess me up too!

For a moment, I felt bad about his girl breaking me off after my parents' death, but now I couldn't care less than two shits if he got his feelings hurt! His girl's shit was weak as hell anyway. I ended up teaching her a few things. Hell, Dickie should have been thanking me for taking away her inhibitions. Mind you, her gold-digging ass told me she didn't care for Dickie Beale anyway. Then she begged me to be her one and only man.

No matter what she said or why she did it, this was messed up. Them fools could've killed me or something. But she was right. It was not her fault. I couldn't blame her although a part of me wanted to.

"Don't cry." I allowed Gabby to leap into my arms. "We're good."

And because I knew I needed her in my life…We were.

Chapter TWENTY-FOUR

It had been more than a week since my birthday. I was all packed and ready for my trip to Vegas with Tin-Can. Once I got back, it would be time to get down to business. First, I had to make a stop.

"Hello, Mama Gwen," I said as I greet Meghan's mom.

"Don't Mama Gwen me," she snarled. "You lost the right to call me that when you pushed Meghan away years ago." Mama Gwen was definitely not pleased with Charlie Mo.

"Then, you had the audacity to hurt my baby again," she continued while folding her arms across her chest.

"Is she here?" I asked.

"No. She went with her father to check on a job at this accounting firm. We think they might give Meghan a chance." Then Mama Gwen started to shut the door.

"Wait...I got something for Meghan."

I reached into my pocket and pulled out a check. I had money once again and plenty of it. But I didn't feel the way I felt the first time. I didn't feel as brash and entitled this time. More than anything, I felt somewhat worried and more cautious.

I knew giving money to Meghan wouldn't fix her pain, but I also knew it might help her to plan a way forward. Plus, I said I would make sure she was okay, so I was there to deliver on that promise.

Mama Gwen took the check out of my hand. "$50,000? You're giving Meghan $50,000?"

"She deserves more than that. Tell her I love her. Tell her to keep her spirits up because she doesn't need a man for anything. Tell her to pull one of her crazy ideas out of that big hard head and go with it."

Surprisingly, Mama Gwen gave me a smile. "I'll tell her just that, Charles."

Tin-Can changed his mind on the Porsche, so I traded it in and got a new Cadillac Escalade. I needed a lot more room without all the glitter anyway.

As soon as I got into my car, I checked my bank account, and there was definitely $1,834,563.64 sitting there. This time I was paying attention to every dime I spent.

But I still had two checks waiting to be cashed. The one I gave Meghan for 50k and the 100k I gave Tin-Can for investments. Once those were settled, I planned to help Gabby with her start-up company.

It took me no more than a minute to forgive Gabby for her connection to those thugs. Yet, I warned her not to associate with those idiots ever again.

***

I didn't plan to spend a lot in Vegas, but of course, I was hoping to bring more money back.

"You ready for your trip?" Gabby asked.

"Yeah."

She kissed me.

"I love you so much. Now go on. I got some cleaning to do."

I looked around Gabby's house. She had junk thrown all over the place.

"You sure do have a mess. Baby, clean this stuff up," I said to her.

"I am. I was throwing away things I didn't need. Out with the old…"

"In with the new," I finished her sentence. "You are your daddy's daughter."

I got an instant call from Tin-Can, so I kissed Gabby again and departed for the airport.

"Let's do this shit!" Tin-Can said as he greeted me. Tin-Can was more excited than I was. My gym buddy, Marcus, decided to tag along.

Tin-Can gave me first-class tickets as a birthday gift. So, I was traveling to Vegas in style.

"Let's meet back here around seven," I said once we made it to the hotel.

My phone died on the flight to Vegas. Once I got it recharged, I noticed a ton of text messages had come through.

I read the ones from Meghan first.

"Why aren't you answering your phone?"

"You didn't have to do this."

"You can have this money back."

"Thank you."

I smiled. I would text Meghan once I got home.

Next, I read the ones from Gabby.

"Have fun."

"I love you."

"I love you so much."

I returned Gabby's texts and said, "I love you too." Then I closed my eyes.

Suddenly, I was awakened by someone beating on the hotel room door. I glanced at my phone.

Damn! I been sleep for two hours.

"Wake your ass up, man! Let's go!" It was Tin-Can!

I pulled myself together and headed out with the fellas. At the end of the night, I had lost over ten-grand.

"Better luck tomorrow, Charlie Mo," Tin-Can laughed as he helped me into my room. I was sloppy drunk.

"Get your drunk ass in the shower," Tin-Can ordered. "I'll see you tomorrow."

I could barely stand, but I bathed as best I could and then went off to bed.

For whatever reason, I couldn't stop thinking about Meghan. So, I decided to give her a call.

But she didn't answer… just as I expected.

***

"There's some kind of big mistake made on my account!" I said to the lady on the phone the next morning. "That check was supposed to be for $100,000. Not $1,100,000."

I checked my statements online only to notice more than a million dollars was gone. Somehow, the bank took out $1,100,000 instead of the $100,000 I signed over to Tin-Can for investments.

"Sir, I was looking at the copy of the check. It hit our bank just yesterday in the amount of $1,100,000. Your personal information on the check matches what we have in the system. After it met all federal regulations, the money was dispersed into three separate venues as requested. Are you saying you didn't write this check out to Stanley Harold?"

"No. That is not what I was saying. Yes, I did write the check. But it was the wrong amount."

"I can see a copy of the check here. It definitely said $1,100,000. Right there in the memo it said *Investments*. Is that correct?"

"As I said, I wrote the check but only for $100,000. Look, I'll go talk to Mr. Harold and call you back."

I slipped on my clothes and rushed to talk to Tin-Can.

As soon as I was in the hallway, I noticed the maid's cart next to Tin-Can's room.

"Excuse me. Where was the man that was in this room?"

"He checked out."

"What? When?"

"I don't know, sir," the maid said.

I knocked on Marcus's door.

"What's up man? You ready to get your gamble on?" Marcus laughed.

"Man. Have you seen Tin-Can?"

"Nah. Not since last night. Why?"

"The maid said he checked out."

"Checked out?!" Marcus shouted.

"Yeah."

Fool Me Thrice

I called Tin-Can's phone. He didn't answer. I told Marcus I was going downstairs.

"Hi! I was checking to see if my friend in room 23213 left a message. The clerk said he checked out, but we weren't scheduled to leave until tomorrow. Stan Harold was his name."

The clerk checked her computer then told me, "Mr. Harold dropped his keys off around 7 o'clock this morning. He said he had to depart early due to a family emergency."

Shit. Something must be wrong.

I called Tin-Can again, but he still didn't pick up.

He's probably on a plane back home.

I called Gabby.

"Hello, is everything alright?"

"No" was all she said. I could tell she had been crying.

"What's wrong? What happened?"

"I love you so much."

"Gabby? What's wrong?"

Gabby didn't respond. She just hung up.

I called her and Tin-Can over and over again before making it back upstairs to Marcus' room. I told him something was wrong with Tin-Can and I wanted to leave.

A few hours later, we were on a plane flying back home. It was almost midnight by the time we arrived in Houston. I went by Gabby's place first, but the house was pitch black. So I headed over to Tin-Can's.

"What the hell?"

There was a SOLD sign in the yard, and the house was deserted. All the blinds were gone. So, I peeped through the windows. It was completely empty. Everything was cleared out except for the oversized chandelier resting on the floor.

I hadn't been to Tin-Can's house since my birthday, but he said nothing about selling his estate.

I tried calling Gabby again.

She didn't pick up, nor did her dad. So, I texted Tin-Can to tell him I was at his house and the place was deserted. I followed up by asking, "Is everything ok?"

Finally, my phone started to vibrate.

Tin-Can!

"Hello man, what's going on? You left Vegas and didn't tell anyone. After I got here, I saw your house was empty, and a SOLD sign was in the yard. Are you okay?"

"Everything is fine...son." Tin-Can's voice was different.

"Okay! So, what was the emergency? Did you get an additional million-dollar deposit with the 100k I gave you?"

Suddenly Tin-Can said, "I got what I was owed."

What the hell was he talking about?

"When I said your father was my brother, he was my brother. Not by blood, but we didn't need blood. We were close. So close, I gave him the money to start his business," said Tin-Can.

"What?" I said.

"It was my money...my drug money from back in the day that got him going. It was the seed that started it all. I helped him become everything he was then he turned on me. He cut me off once he started making real clean money.

"I remember the day everything changed between us. I asked him to help me go legit. But guess what? That bastard told me 'No.' He told me I'd made enough money selling drugs where I should be able to start my own shit. He said I should've been smarter. Yet, he wasn't saying all of that bullshit when I kept him afloat. Nor did he say that when I adopted his love child."

"What the hell are you saying, Stan?"

"Violet is your sister, Charlie Mo. But she doesn't know that. Hell, even Gabby was too young to remember her mama not being pregnant."

"Stan, what the hell are you talking about? I was my daddy's only child!"

"No, son. You're not. That woman got pregnant on your daddy. She was about to mess up his marriage and his business reputation. So, I paid that gold-digger off with my damn money, and I took in Violet at one-month-old. I told your father not to worry because I took care of everything for him. My wife wanted another baby anyway. Vicki was having problems conceiving at the time. Then along came Violet. Problem solved!"

I didn't know what to say. I was just dumbfounded. But Tin-Can continued on.

"There wasn't a damn thing I wouldn't have done for your dad. But after adopting Violet, I hit rock bottom. The streets weren't what they used to be. Yes, I put money up for my kids just like he did for you, but I wasn't going to touch that. So, I asked my brother for a loan. Just a little something to tide me over until I was back on my feet.

"He was getting plenty of shine, and his name was starting to ring bells. But he turned his back on me. He told me to get a job. Of course, I did. Thank God. But he screwed over the wrong person. It was always the S-O-B that doesn't have a pot to piss in that wants to make the biggest splash!

"He started out with shit, then suddenly he was pissing on me. I never forgave him. I figured out how to made my little money work for me. Yes, my holdings bought me that house and took care of my family, including your daddy's child.

"But lately, my investments have hit a wall. They are not producing what they used to. So, all that investment shit I was selling you was a load of crap. I knew I could make you want more. Just like I talked your daddy into going after more. You're just like him. You see, I had my daughter get close to you. I sent Gabby your way. I told her your family wronged her family a long time ago, and I needed her next to you."

"Gabby was in on this shit too?" I don't know why I asked.

"More or less. She doesn't know all the basics. But she knew I needed her as close to you as possible for my own personal reasons. What better way than being your love interest? You see, Charlie Mo, my girls don't have sex for free. You had money potential. So, I told her I really favored you over any of those other poor bastards that wanted her. I taught my kids how to do wrong the right way."

I was just sick to my stomach. Literally.

Surprisingly, Tin-Can showed a tad bit of remorse. "Like a fool, Gabby fell in love with you. She wasn't supposed to. Hell, has been crying all day because she had to let you go."

I was heated. I really wanted to beat some asses.

Fool Me Thrice

"I do like you, son..."

"I'm not your goddamn son!"

"This wasn't about you or our relationship. This was about what I was owed. All I needed to do was wait on your trust fund to kick in. No matter what amount you wrote on that check, I had a way to make sure it said what I needed it to say. I was owed this from your daddy. Not to mention half of that money he left you belonged to Violet anyway. You even blew her share. Your daddy knew of Violet and never offered us one brown penny. So, I took what was owed to us. Now, your daddy and me are all settled. Even Steven.

"Your daddy caused this. He was a sucker. A disgrace. A stingy, uppity-acting, no good, son-of-a-bastard. Plus, a horrible father."

"You son-of-a-bitch," was all I could muster.

Tin-Can still wasn't letting up.

"Your dad could make money, but he wasn't shit as a human, and you know it. He ain't teach you shit. Not even common sense. Not even as much sense as he had. He would have seen the hustle a mile away, but you didn't. You just wanted to be seen. Loved. I gave you what you needed. My family gave you what you needed until I got what I wanted out of you.

"As for you, Charlie Mo, you should have learned from the first or second gold-digger. But no, just like your father, you were a senseless sucker. That paperwork I had you sign last night while you were drinking...well, it was a bunch of bullshit. You barely paid attention to it because you trusted me. So, take me to court if you must, but that paperwork will tell my story. Trust me. It was legally binding. You wouldn't be able to get shit!"

Tin-Can played me. Gabby played me.

"My family and I have gone hundreds of miles away to start over. You should do the same. I left you more than enough money. Take that money and use it like I taught you. On a lighter note, I am sure you remember not seeing me at your parents' burial. Well, that was when I took that beautiful chandelier. You can have it back now. I didn't have enough room to take it with me. But whatever you do going forward, don't get hustled again. Goodbye… son."

With that, Tin-Can hung up and left me in eerie silence. Out of shock, anger, and embarrassment, I called him right back, but he didn't answer. So, I started to blow up Gabby's phone.

I couldn't believe she and Tin-Can turned out to be just like everyone else. Money-hungry gold-diggers. They all took my promiscuity for weakness while knowing all they wanted was money from me.

I was hurt. Shit. It really screwed me up. N

The first five times I called Gabby, I got no answer. But the sixth time, I got the automated message telling me the number was no longer in service.

She was gone. Tin-Can was gone. I was out of over a million dollars and all alone. Again.

I started driving toward my apartment in complete silence.

They hustled the shit out of me.

There wasn't a damn thing I can do about it. Like Tin-Can said, I had no idea what I signed last night. I was drinking, and I was surprised he had the paperwork in his pocket. I remember putting my name on a document and just giving it back to him.

Fool Me Thrice

Obviously, I was fooled and played by Gabby. She drew me in and stepped on my heart like mashed potatoes. Then, Tin-Can made a fool out of me while pretending to be a friend, a mentor, and a father figure while manipulating me for his own financial revenge. Finally, I completely fooled myself by thinking I was getting what I wanted with the ladies I dated, yet I failed to see how gullible those relationships made me for Gabby and Tin Can.

Maybe, Gabby didn't know what her father was up to, but she knew he was up to something. She was doing whatever he told her to do. Damn!

I will never trust another woman ever again. I can't believe I have a sister. Someone that shares my Daddy's blood.

Violet was right in my face for months, and I didn't know who she was to me. I was still trying to process my dad having a child by someone else. Dad professed so much love for my mom while she was warning him about women with bad intentions. But I never thought daddy was sleeping around. He betrayed my mom and abandoned me in some ways too.

Soon, I arrived at my apartment building, but it took me forever to get out of the car. My mind was all screwed up. I was sick and tired of my life being full of disappointments.

Finally, I forced myself out of my ride and walked inside. I opened my apartment door. As soon as I turned on the lights, I noticed an envelope at my feet with my name on it.

I opened the envelope, and it was my $50,000 check from Meghan along with a letter.

"I never wanted your money. Just you. I loved you for you, and no amount of money will ever change that. I could have been poor and hungry as long as I was poor and hungry with you. So, I didn't need your *check. I'll find my own way, and I hope you find yours too. I'll always love you. Meghan."*

It's her.

All along, it had been Meghan.

This was the woman I was supposed to be with. This was the woman I need by my side. This was the woman I needed to get through the rest of my life.

It's Meghan.

It always had been.

Chapter TWENTY-FIVE

Dean Conan

*T*wo *months later...*

If this didn't go as planned, I was out of $20,000 and no woman.

For the past two months, I've been working through my anger, getting over Gabby and the shit Tin-Can did to me. I've been in full grind mode. With the little money I had left, I could still made a few things happen.

My business, Charlie Mo' Pack & Go Moving Company, was up and running. It was mine, all mine. I did change the name and logo, though. The hell with Gabby and her fake ass gesture!

I had two trucks, but I was still working out of my house. I guessed that I would be able to secure a building real soon as long as business stayed the way it was. Three weeks after my grand opening, I had more than enough jobs to kept me busy. I was so proud of myself.

However, I had just spent 20k, and it wasn't on my business, either. I had invested it into Meghan's wedding that she had absolutely no idea about; it was all part of my plan to win her back.

I was very nervous, but I had organized a team to help pull it off.

"Charlie Mo? What are you doing here?"

I had been standing outside of Meghan's job, waiting for her to show.

Meghan's boss liked my idea, so he wasn't expecting her back at work. I got lucky and persuaded the office, Meghan's friends, and her family to go along with my proposal. After hearing my plea, everyone got on board to help me win Meghan's heart. It wasn't easy, but I promised them a real fairytale ending.

I haven't seen nor heard from Gabby and Tin-Can. But I didn't really care except for the money I lost. No one knows where they are. They're just gone. I couldn't even find them on social media.

Fool Me Thrice

I tried speaking to a lawyer, but he needed to know more about the document I signed. He said a copy of the check would be my word against Tin-Can's. So, I didn't have much of a choice except to let it go. But if Meghan would be my bride, then the healing would be easier with her by my side.

"I have to get back to work," Meghan said while trying to walk past me.

I reached out to grab her by the arm.

"It was always you. You were right in front of my face for all these years. It was always you."

After Meghan returned my check with her heartfelt letter, I was forced to realize she was "the one" all along. She was definitely my soulmate.

"What are you talking about?" Meghan asked.

"No woman has ever cared about me the way you have. No one has ever looked out for me or loved me like you. Living with you was easy, genuine, kind, and simple. You were more than enough, but I was too stupid to see it.

I can tell Meghan was touched by my words.

"Please take my hand."

"What?"

"I've already spoken to your boss. Trust me. Teddy knows. Meghan, please take my hand!"

"My boss knows what, Charlie Mo?"

I reached for Meghan's hand once again.

"What? Where are we going?"

We started to walk down the sidewalk.

The church was literally right down the street from her job.

"Remember when we used to walk around my neighborhood?"

"I remember," Meghan responded.

"So many times, I wanted to kiss you back in high school. I wanted to be the reason for your smiles. I wanted to be the glare on the other side of those glasses. But I was afraid. Since you were capable of whipping my ass, I didn't dare to approach you in that manner. But I always knew there was much more to you. I knew you were more than a hard-ass tomgirl. The way you talked and the way you laughed made me secretly adore you. I've always admired everything about you." Meghan smirked while I continued marching toward the church.

"I know I messed up. I know I've hurt you so many times before, but never again. Let me start anew. Allow me the chance to spend the rest of my life making it all up to you."

Suddenly, I stopped right in front of the church, so she could see her family, the decorations, and the glam squad just waiting for her arrival. Meghan could see the beauty of this moment was bigger than the pain of our past.

"Charlie Mo, what are you doing?"

Right then and there, I got down on one knee and held Meghan's hand. There were screams of approval echoing from blocks away.

"I know I hurt you. I know I let you down time and time again. I can only imagine how you felt when I didn't pick you, but I'm man enough to admit I failed you. I failed us!"

"Charlie Mo..."

Fool Me Thrice

"Meghan, let me finish. Now I realize how much you loved me. I want you to know how much I love you too. I want to spend the rest of my life loving you, Meghan Fuller."

"You called me what? You called me Meghan Fuller!!!"

While I was still holding Meghan's hand, I pulled out the ring box.

"I'm not a perfect man. No, not at all. I can be stupid, stubborn, confused, and unsure. But I know one thing. I know there's no other woman in this world more perfect for me than you."

I opened the box so Meghan could see my three-carat ring.

"So, Meghan Monaid Montgomery, will you be my dream come true? Will you do me the honor of making me the happiest man in the world by becoming my wife? I know it may sound crazy. I know we haven't talked in months. I know we stopped on bad terms, but I mean every word I'm saying to you. Meghan, will you marry me?"

Meghan was breathing so hard I thought she was going to pass out.

"Charlie Mo, what are you doing? Why are you doing this?" Meghan started to cry.

"I'm doing this because I love you. I'm doing this because I can't live without you. I'm doing this because I need you. I don't care how crazy or weak I look. Meghan, I'm not giving up without a fight!

"Even your mother and father approve of this. We've all been waiting for you. Look at them. They want you to say yes. I told them how much I love you. We just need a yes, dear!"

Meghan was crying so uncontrollably that her body begins to shake.

"I got you. I promise. Just like you had me all those years, I got you. All you have to do was say yes."

While looking into Meghan's eyes, I could tell she was still afraid and unsure.

"This isn't just a proposal. This is also your wedding day! I a, not waiting! I want to make you mine today. I had everything planned out. Your sister helped me pick out your wedding gown. Everything is ready. All you have to do is say yes. Your family, friends, and co-workers will be here at 4 o'clock. The church is ready. The flowers, the food, and everything needed is all here. All you have to do was say yes to being my wife."

Megan took a deep breath then gave me a smile I'd never seen before.

"Charlie Mo, this is the craziest and most romantic thing that has ever happened to me."

"I know this is crazy. I know. But I am crazy about you. I spent the past two months preparing myself for only you. I'm ready. All you have to do is say yes."

Then suddenly, Meghan started to nod.

"Oh God! Yes, Charlie Mo! Yes," she said. " I'll marry you!"

I was smiling so hard my eyes were slightly closed. I twisted the ring on Meghan's finger and stood up to kiss the woman who was going to be my wife. I kiss the woman who I was going to be with for the rest of my life. I couldn't be happier!

I'd been through hell. I'd been through a lot since the loss of my folks. Yet, pound for pound, I was my own destruction in the flesh. I can even say I was mentally dead without Meghan. I met so many different types of money-hungry women and so many users. I definitely lost count.

Along the way, I have discovered all women aren't the same. Yes, women do lie. Yes, women do cheat too. But my friends and relatives have lied and deceived me more than any gold-digger.

But this time, I have secured a good friend and a good woman. I have a real one this time. Someone who has loved me since the very beginning. Someone who loved me before I knew how to love myself.

Meghan was created just for me. Now, she is all mine.

As I look toward the heavens, I know my parents are so proud of me and my decision to marry this amazing woman.

I'm now the man I was always destined to be and not the three-timing fool I became. I was the son of Charles Theodore Fuller. Always was. Always will be.

The End.

Dean Conan

ABOUT THE AUTHOR

Conan Steele:

Conan grew up in Atlanta, Georgia with a single mom and an absent father. It was his relationship with his mother that strengthen his character as a gentleman. His mother moonlighted as a blues singer during his early years. She would take little Conan to night clubs as her way of working and kept an eye on her son. It was these seedy bars that inspired Conan to go into show-business. When Hollywood failed to take him in, he tried to break into the modeling industry. Yet, Conan didn't have quite the physique nor the flair to remain in Men Fashion, so he took to the mic as a comic. It didn't take long for Conan to find out being in comedy wasn't his niche either. Since Conan wasn't a fit for Broadway, he decided to pick up a pen and write fictional stories about his love life, friendships, and international travels.

Printed in Great Britain
by Amazon

4d9a5c7d-5f7b-4a91-acc2-1ae16ea43cb3R01